THE PROXIMITY OF STARS

BENEDICT STUART

*To people who would like to rediscover themselves and the
world.*

THROUGHOUT THE HISTORY OF HUMAN CIVILIZATION there have been numerous occasions of recorded golden ages across empires, states, nationalities and cultures.

Most people around the world have always wanted to live a better life here on Earth. Nevertheless, only a few have ever believed it has been at all possible in their lifetimes.

Even nowadays, people still aspire to the same dream, despite turmoil and confusion spreading around the globe.

This story will take you on an adventure into the future, half a century or so ahead, attempting to predict some likely scenarios of human development. A company of a few strong female characters is introduced as a precursor to bright prospects on the path of hope.

Also included are several solutions to modern ills, in order for us to get closer to today's dream of a better society tomorrow.

[1]

21ST CENTURY, PLANET EARTH
ST. ANASTASIA ISLAND
SUMMERTIME

IT WAS NEARING SUNSET WHEN THE SKY SLOWLY turned amber. Brian could see two seagulls wafting on the golden horizon. The island seemed rather cozy for the two young and hopeful lads who just wanted to unwind a bit before entering into the world of hard work, family life and eventually, kids.

Having graduated from Oxbridge with flying colors, both Brian and his best friend, Gary, were willing to experience something new, unfamiliar and fascinating. Gary was the wilder one, far more adventurous than Brian, who was generally regarded as a profound thinker.

In fact, he was renowned, or rather, notorious, for constantly having his head in the clouds – the so-called "philosopher" not only in their posh college, but also the entire varsity.

Right after their graduation ball, these two young

men had to fly several thousand miles in order to come to this tiny, yet splendid and surreal patch of land, right off the coast of Southeastern Europe.

Little did they know what lay ahead of them. So full of dreams, enthusiasm, and naiveté, they were ill-prepared to go on to the next stage of their existence.

Brian got up from the hot sand and took a look at the magnificent sunset. Just then, he noticed something rather unusual for this sleepy island.

"Gary, could you come over here for a second?" he asked his travel companion.

"Are you afraid of the dark or what?" Gary replied in his typical jovial style, as he approached Brian, standing right next to the water of the Black Sea.

"Oh, Brian, stop philosophizing so much and grab a can of beer, or one of your favorite glasses of wine!" Gary teased.

"Bro, I'm tellin' ya, I was just wondering if we're gonna like the local cuisine here, when I heard an odd kinda sound from—er, like—"

Suddenly, he stopped in mid-sentence.

In came a soft, chirpy, somewhat flirtatious female greeting: "Hey, guys, are you two having fun?"

"Good evening, alien beauty. How the heck did you manage to get here, in this secluded place?" Gary responded quickly, eyeing her up and down, appreciatively.

Gary's mood started to improve significantly. "Never mind, that doesn't really matter right now, does it, Brian?" He turned to the girl. "Anyways, now that you are here one way or another, would you like to share a drink with us and keep us company?"

"You are so-oo pushy, you naughty young man," replied the stranger, giggling, "Let me first introduce myself properly. My name's Brenda, and that, over there by the beach, is my best friend Alice."

Much to their amazement, none of the guys had yet sensed the presence of Alice—until that instant.

Brisk and eager introductions ensued between the boys and the girls, with Gary, himself, literally exploding with excitement and delight.

Prior to the ladies' arrival, he had been feeling cold, lonely, and slightly bored with the prospect of spending a quiet and uneventful night in his friend's unassuming company. But then came this delightful surprise.

"We went on a cruise today, starting off from the city of Burgas first thing in the morning," Brenda said. "Accidentally, we spotted this nice little islet and immediately wanted to check it out. Because we thought there might be a tavern or at least a café on this beach or something, our desire to explore further didn't diminish, so we went on to—"

Gary interrupted her with a smirk. "Oh, Brenda, hm, er, please be our guests for tonight. We are really nice guys, very smart, intelligent and hospitable."

While he went on smoothly talking to the gals, Gary motioned for them to follow him into the villa, where dinner had already been properly prepared by the kitchen staff, now gone for the night.

"All right then, ladies, do feel at home and enjoy your meal. *Bon appetit*! There's plenty of food for all of us here," he said. "Besides, we've got a fully stocked fridge as well, not to mention the minibar, which has also been completely restocked recently."

While reaching out to light the candles on the large dinner table, Gary beamed.

"Hey, Brian, could you now put some lovely music on, please?" he asked.

"Yeah, sure mate, of course, just a moment," Brian replied courteously. Yet his face and voice indicated otherwise, as if he were concealing his true feelings so he didn't spoil his friend's potentially romantic evening.

The Moon's pallid face had just shown up on the skyline. With the close proximity of Mars shining brightly, and the gentle ripples of water splashing against the fine golden sand, the entire scene looked incredible.

[2]

THE TWO SLENDER GIRLS SEEMED LIKE A "GODSEND",
like eye candy to Gary. He carried on chatting eagerly
with them over dinner. The Mediterranean food was
quite appetizing and delicious. The seafood dishes and
side orders went extremely well with a bottle of white
wine.

"So, Brenda, how do you find this snug little house
right in the middle of nowhere?" Gary continued
blatantly.

"Well, it's a great place to be, especially with you
guys, of course," Brenda retorted with a sparkle in her
eyes.

"Sorry, but I can't help asking why you both are
stuck here, being so lonely. You're both straight after
all, aren't you?"

"Oh, this is our after-party, in fact. We've just graduated, you see," Brian jumped in, looking slightly perplexed at Brenda.

"Good heavens! You can talk then," Alice replied in
turn.

"Of course I can, I simply couldn't get a word in
edgeways the whole evening, because of my friend Gary,
the chatterbox. And, just look who's telling me I didn't

dare to speak, you sneaky snake in the grass," Brian responded in a seemingly agitated way.

Gary looked surprised.

"All right, all right, calm down and stay cool, you two," Brenda insisted with urgency. "I was only teasing you, so please excuse me and accept my sincere apologies. I didn't mean to offend you in any way. You both seem like really nice guys, rather adorable, to be honest. I even suppose you have a bunch of admiring ladies chasing after you, right Gary?

"On second thought, I wonder if you were trying to escape from some wildcats, tigresses, bimbos or something?" Brenda was obviously attempting to make up in a more amicable manner.

Alice cut in, "Brian and Gary, if you allow me to say a few words as well. We really didn't want to cause any hassle to you by popping up like that, unannounced. We could leave this instant, if you wish."

Brian replied, "No, no, Alice, of course that's out of the question. We don't want you to leave now in the middle of the night. We're nice blokes after all – real gentlemen, so to speak."

Brian was visibly more cooperative and ready to negotiate, "As we said before, you're most welcome, ladies! Please enjoy your stay here with us. May I therefore kindly ask you to a dance? It'll be an honor for me. I can even hear a pleasant ballad playing in the background, as we speak."

"I can't agree with you more, sir," Alice replied. "What a brilliant idea, thank you." She grabbed Brian's offered hand, smiling.

A few seconds later, there were two dancing couples on the improvised dance floor next to the bar counter-top, bopping and swaying in time to the sweet melody.

The state of peace and quiet was restored and ruled harmoniously for the next four or five minutes. Everything seemed very tranquil and appeasing. The gentle music was the only thing that could now be heard in the house. Both girls and boys appeared to be relishing the soft, swinging moves to the rhythm of the blues.

The roar of the surf could also be heard, as though the waves were following the sound of music.

When the song ended, Gary returned to his usual cheerful but sort of smarmy manner. "Girls, since it's getting late now, would you like me to show you to your bedroom? As your considerate host, I'd be glad to welcome you on board once again and put you up for this memorable night."

Gary's cheeks had turned crimson, not due to embarrassment, but because he had already emptied several glasses of wine. Apparently, he was not much of a drinker.

Sensing his growing desire and considering the allusions made, Brenda quickly regained her composure. "That's very kind of you, Gary. However, I suppose you've got some big plans for tomorrow. Don't tell me you're going to stay in bed all day, having a lie-in?"

Gary understood the irony in her intonation but did not want to back off and resign like a loser just yet.

"We could actually enjoy your lovely company for a little longer tomorrow and go out together on a city tour, if you like. We definitely want to be out and about during our vacation, what do you say?"

Brenda glanced at Brian, her eyes begging for help.

"Gary, let's behave ourselves and leave the ladies alone now. We'll talk to them again in the morning for sure, when seeing them off, okay man?"

After a second of silence, and without any more verbal objections, Brian helped Gary stand up and go to his bed. He urgently needed to speak to him and express his concerns about the ladies as quietly and as tactfully as possible.

But the moment his head hit the pillow, Gary fell fast asleep and began snoring in between blabbering some drunken gibberish.

"The night brings counsel," murmured Brian.

By then his face had become sharp and serious again, but he forced himself to look polite before going back downstairs to attend to the suspicious girls.

"Sorry about my friend's behavior earlier tonight. We've been to some wild parties lately and he hasn't got, I mean, gotten over them yet, obviously. Let me take you to your room now; please follow me."

"Ah, don't even mention it, big boy. We're glad we landed on this lovely little island, Mr. Sunderland," Brenda tried to reassure Brian in an overly flirtatious way.

Brian's fearsome apprehensions came over him once again at full throttle.

"And how do you happen to know my surname then, Brenda?" Brian was lost for words and steaming under his stern facade.

"Calm down and take it easy, young man! The tour guide told us about you and your friend when we got off the cruise boat earlier today," Alice explained. "In fact, we are extraordinary dancers and could perform for your eyes only, Brian. The night is still young and—"

Alice leaned toward Brian's face and attempted a sly but gentle kiss on the verge of his mouth, just below his now-rosy cheek. Brian shivered a bit, instinctively recoiling and backing away.

"Look ladies, I really don't want to be rude, but I actually don't know you. That's why you should let me make something clear." Brian paused for a second or so to gather his racing thoughts. "Now, not that I am supposed to explain anything to you at all, but at some point tonight you seemed like fairly decent ladies."

"Wha-aat, what do you mean by 'decent'? What are

you implying here? Do you think we are some sort of sluts, pickpockets or gold seekers, Mr. Right? And what kinda word's that, by the way, who says 'decent' nowadays; did your granny or grandpa use it, hey-ho?" Brenda retaliated quite cheekily.

Then Brian got the idea, the whole picture was now crystal clear, no doubt at all. The only glitch was that he was in two minds as to whether he should chuck those two little bitches out straight away by calling the coast guards in the middle of the night or just "tell the girls off", take them in and then go to bed himself.

Shortly afterwards, he made up his mind. He decided to be a genteel guy, as usual, although he subconsciously knew he might bitterly regret his choice later on.

If, by any chance, the worst comes to the worst, then they couldn't pose any threat, could they? By all means, they're leaving in the morning.

"OK, Alice and Brenda, I do apologize for my misdemeanor, but you definitely need to leave at dawn; do we have a deal?"

The girls appeared more cooperative now and nodded in consent. Brian felt a bit less tense and continued: "I'll arrange a water taxi boat for you, if you need one."

"Don't bother. I've got my smartphone with me, so we can arrange it ourselves," Alice quickly retorted.

"Very well then, here's your room. There are a couple of spare bedsheets in the chest. Good night ladies and farewell to you both."

The two girls did as instructed. They even seemed a bit too obedient to Brian. Needless to say, his mind was boggling. He realized he had just shot himself in the foot. He had to have a word with his best friend Gary, because things had just got out of hand. But, should he wake him up this very moment, or wait until daybreak?

Let's not get paranoid! Gary's still drunk, and besides, there's nothing to be afraid of, is there?

Finally, Brian went to bed and, almost immediately after that, sleep got the better of him. It had been a long day for the young boys.

[3]

MEANWHILE, IN THE GIRLS' BEDROOM CHITCHAT WAS rife. The night was really sultry, so the ladies couldn't fall asleep. By the look of it, they weren't going to sleep a wink until dawn.

"Brian's a cool and awesome guy. I really regret accepting this mission." Alice was speaking her mind.

"Now, that's something new. Are you experiencing some kind of soul-searching or a feeling of remorse?" Brenda snapped at Alice ruthlessly.

"Don't forget that's the brother of Dixon, the World President, the bastard that nobody likes. The universal dictator, the one that we'll eventually have to deal with. I wish we could wipe him out from the face of the earth one day.

"Thus, we'll save not only our precious planet, but also the newly acquired human colonies like the Moon, Mars, the upcoming Venus project and, last but not least, the International Space Station (ISS). The latter, at present, is a megapolis for the filthy rich holiday-makers and affluent retirees, bless 'em all!"

"You shouldn't speak so openly about your true feelings for Dixon. His hounds, that is, bozos, might be snooping around as we discuss those nasty things," Alice interrupted.

"What, in this godforsaken place? Come on, Alice! And just look who's telling me this, the very lover of Mr. Big Brother, who ain't so much into women altogether."

"Brenda, stop right there, don't you dare! You've got absolutely no idea how hard my life as a poor orphan has been so far. And what's more, Dixon was like family to me. Now, back to your stupid query: who was flirting shamelessly with both Gary and Brian tonight, huh?"

At that precise moment, while still dark outside, there was a sudden but faint noise, which could be heard in the distance. It apparently sounded like a military chopper, fast approaching in a menacing manner.

"Hush, hush Alice, we need to make our way out of here immediately, as quietly as possible," Brenda ordered nervously and the two spy girls were gone in a matter of seconds, literally.

Their room looked neat and tidy, as if nobody had slept inside that night.

———

The threatening sound of a nearing helicopter was now loud and clear; even the house was being rhythmically shaken. Arguably, the whole little island was being shattered. Right then, Gary opened his sleepy eyes.

"What the hell's that?" he asked, his voice conveying a great deal of annoyance, irritation and frustration, but without any hint of anxiety or concern.

"What exactly do you mean, old-timer?" Brian tried to open his eyes too, still not quite aware of the situation.

"I thought we were supposed to stay in a nice and quiet villa by the sea, weren't we? I'll certainly complain about that and ask for a refund," Gary was now startled and shaken to the core, but wanted to appear well composed, even witty.

"Are you sure you aren't bearing the fruits of your hangover, buddy?" Brian retorted accordingly, but right after that his croaky voice was drowned out by the thunderous touchdown of an enormous chopper, just in front of the house, on the edge of the nicely manicured lawn.

This was a scary sight by itself. The boys couldn't believe their eyes. All that seemed so unreal. They wished they were dreaming. Unfortunately, their alleged nightmare turned out to be the reality they had never even anticipated.

Several minutes later there were about a dozen armed to the teeth troopers, all set in line, eagerly awaiting someone undoubtedly very important to get out of the helicopter.

Quite right. A moment later, the one and only General Grant, the Commander-in-Chief of Dixon's Planetary Army, turned up on the chopper's steps.

His figure was imposing. Destiny was not at all favorable to the unlucky bastards who had the chance to catch a glimpse of this infamous general. Most of them were not among the living anymore.

[4]

"GARY, HURRY UP FOR GOD'S SAKE, LET'S GET OUTTA here before these guerrillas ram into the house."

"Alright bro, if you assume this could save our damned lives somehow."

"Gary, cut the crap; don't be so daft, will you? We haven't done anything wrong, right? Only those two tarts last night were freaking suspicious, but I don't think . . ."

"Oh, right, are they still around then, I mean the two beauties, Brian?"

"No, I'm sure they're gone now, as I instructed."

"As you did what? Are you insane? To kick those bombshells out, are you straight?"

"Gary, yes, I'm straight, OK. Now, calm down and let's get things sorted with the Death General outside first. He's my wicked brother Dixon's right hand, but I'm sure we can solve whatever there is in a civilized manner."

"I really doubt that Brian—just take a look at their big guns, ready to shoot without any remorse."

"Are you a wimp, a chicken, or a pussy, Gary? Get yourself together and let's face the challenge, shall we?"

Then, Brian opened the front door resolutely and without a hint of hesitation.

"Good mo-oorning, gentlemen! Good morn, General Grant. How can we help you, sir? What made you come here, if I may ask?"

"Your hands up, you two scumbags. Now, shall I repeat, dumbheads? Don't keep the Law waiting," one of the officers barked histrionically, his loaded gun pointing at them unambiguously.

"Alright, alright, we haven't done anything wrong, have we?" Gary tried to explain.

"Could you tell us what's going on here? You should be aware that both my parents are high-ranking military lawyers and are going to sue you for assault if you carry on that way."

Smack, swoosh, punch, crash, bang, boom, stomp, thud.

The tough officer pushed Gary down to the ground with quite a few heavy but swift punches. Gary felt an excruciating pain in the cheekbones and they started bleeding immediately afterwards.

"You pathetic bastards, you downright cowards, I will—"

A couple of the remaining officers handcuffed Gary and got a firm hold of him, then dragged him toward the roaring chopper.

"Get inside the damn house now and search it all over, you bunch of lazy morons," the General commanded, his voice sounding like a thunderstorm, even louder than the sound of the powerful helicopter's engine.

Six or seven officers ran up and down the house, rummaging about and throwing nearly anything outside in a disorderly manner. Needless to say, the summer villa turned into a complete wreck a few minutes later.

Brian stood motionless, speechless, and dumbfounded.

Suddenly, General Grant approached and sidled up to him in somewhat amicable way. "Dear boy," he started off, "I know who you are and I really regret to tell you, but you and your friend are in a deep mess. There have been serious charges pressed against you and your accomplice, so to say. You're both accused of espionage and conspiracy against our President."

"Hold on a second, General. Did Dick, sorry, Dixon, my own so-called brother, send you down here? Excuse me, but I personally haven't seen him for ages. In fact, ever since my late mother Annette Fleming and his late father divorced.

"Come on, General, you know that quite well. You also served in the armed forces at the time when my late granddad, my mum's father, Peter Drake was General of the World Army, as I was told.

"There must've been an enormous mistake. I mean, Dixon and I live thousands of miles away from each other and our paths have never crossed ever since our parents divorced."

"Look Brian, it doesn't matter what I think or know. I simply have to obey and carry out orders, you see. Therefore, I beg you to cooperate, my son, for your own sake." The General's voice conveyed some hints of hesitation.

"General, don't call this rubbish your son, will you? He's nobody's son. His mother was a damn whore—"

Mr. Vince Brandon, the Minister of World Defense, popped out from the chopper in his shiny high-tech protective uniform, cursing away at Brian and his deceased mother.

"What did you just call my mother, Mr. Coward?" asked Brian. Now he was blue in the face.

"Wow, looks who's talking? The little son of a bitch dares to speak to me in such an indignant fashion. I shall order my men to shut your dirty mouth this very moment for good."

General Grant motioned Brian to calm down and

keep quiet, but to no avail. Unfortunately, it was rather too late already.

Brian had already leapt forward like a young, but less experienced, cougar and was currently attempting to bash Mr. Brandon in the face, disregarding the strong metal gear the latter was wearing. Despite that such a course of action seemed a lost cause, Brian was prepared to resort to fisticuffs.

To everyone's amazement, a few seconds later Vince was wriggling from embarrassment rather than pain caused by the several good punches to his uncovered face. He even sported a few bruises and scratches. There were just a few drops of blood trickling down, almost invisibly.

On the other hand, Brian's knuckles looked seriously injured by the metal plates of Vince's outfit, which Brian so ferociously had been trying to smash. The outcome was his own dripping blood.

"Stop him now. Restrain this looney bastard, this tiny little sod," Vince shouted at the top of his lungs.

At that exact instant, three or four officers laid their hands on Brian and pulled him down, getting him off Mr. Brandon. However, instead of just apprehending him, right after he touched the ground, they started ruthlessly kicking him with their military boots.

Several minutes later, Brian had almost lost consciousness, thinking he was dying in anguish.

Then the Minister spoke again and gave an order: "Stop, we need him alive for now; even though I'd be extremely happy if he died right here, on the spot."

Hence, the officers ceased their attack, as instructed.

Vince went up to Brian and looked him in his now murky blue eyes.

"You little piece of shit, how could you even think of beating me?"

Then he raised his right hand, holding a metal bar in

the form of a truncheon, and hit Brian so hard that Brian yelped with pain. His mouth started sprinkling blood all over and he had to spew out both of his upper incisors.

"Don't ever dare to call me a coward, you midget. Glad I taught you a lesson. Do you realize who I am? Now, I believe you won't be able to speak with this filthy mouth of yours the rest of your miserable life. Your time's rapidly running out, anyways: tick-tock, tick-tock."

Brian collapsed and fainted, hitting the rough ground. The patch of grass around him turned brownish-red.

"Hurry. Take him inside the chopper and let's get outta this smelly dump," Vince yelled.

"No, just a moment, Minister," the General objected.

Vince looked at him in astonishment.

"Please, hold on a second, guys," he repeated, "we haven't read them their rights, plus we haven't even mentioned the actual accusations, formally, so to speak."

Apparently, the General was stalling for time.

"Oh General, don't be so old-fashioned. I think we're all done with that crap."

"I don't want to object to you, Mr. Brandon but, as the President commanded, we need to give 'em a choice. I'm certain you remember that quite well, sir."

"So, what's the point?" The Minister was beginning to lose his temper, not mentioning his non-existent patience.

Sensing that, the General pointed at Gary, who had been sitting silently, befuddled, inside the chopper.

"You know, his parents could theoretically sue us afterwards, unless we follow the procedures diligently. Bearing in mind they are top lawyers at the President's Office."

"I doubt they would even bother to inquire about their criminal son from now on. But if you insist, General, go on; tell the brat what he's guilty of, provided you can wake up the sleepy little monster first, of course. Just take a look at his pants; he'd surely wetted them all over by now, ha-ha!"

By that time, the Sun had appeared on the horizon.

[5]

BRIAN FELT SOMEONE THROW COLD WATER IN HIS FACE and slowly started opening his heavy eyes. The pain in his mouth recurred in full-force and he grimaced. Then, he started squealing and whimpering like a badly hurt dog. At that moment, he saw the General ordering one of the officers to bring in some painkillers from the chopper's first-aid kit. Despite the fast, soothing effect of the painkillers, Brian didn't feel any better. In fact, the General had to give Brian an injection in the shoulder so that he could recuperate from the shock.

"Listen Brian, I'm afraid you don't have too many options at present. You either plead guilty and go to jail for life, or otherwise, you'll be exiled to the Moon. If you're lucky, those will be your best-case scenarios, to be honest."

The General was about to begin one of his favorite long-winded lectures, when Brian summoned the strength to talk. "I really doubt Dixon, the freaking demon, will let me live long behind bars. On top of that, he's recently reintroduced the death penalty across the globe. In contrast, going to the Moon to live with some ancient shadows of people, who keep records of events long passed, wouldn't be an option I'd consider viable. I'd better die than live with the half-dead, zombie-like folks there. Today's perhaps one of my darkest days, if not the last one, General—but thanks for your concern." Brian finally paused to take a deep breath, as it took him great pains to continue. His speech sounded like a mumble due to his toothless mouth. His jaw was sticking out like an eyesore.

"You see, my boy, the darkest hour's just before the dawn. Life's a precious gift we all need to cherish at any given time and age. Think carefully, coz you won't have much time left on your hands afterwards. Can you see the news bulletin being displayed on the interactive billboard right down by the beacon?

"They're shouting out about you and your friend Gary, showing your mugshots as though you're some sort of unnamed terrorists, villains, some people of no importance. Many would be looking forward to seeing you both being lynched."

"Stop chatting, General. Don't you remember how we were being briefed," Vince cut out their conversation, "there's really no point in that. After all, we don't even know those two crooks by any means. You see, General, my men searched the entire house and couldn't find any ID cards or proof of identity whatsoever."

He continued after a short pause. "Evidently, those two rascals aren't carrying any personal documents on them either, as they're still in their swimsuits or underwear, by the look of it. In the meantime, we've already carried out some DNA tests and there appears to be no evidence of their current existence according to the Government's Centralized Database. Therefore, General, you can't be at all sure you're talking to Brian. This young bastard might well be a bloody impostor, you know." Vince was grinning complacently.

The grim prospects dawned on Brian at that moment. Life seemed to be sucking so hopelessly for him and his best friend Gary.

"Furthermore, we found evidence that these two nasty pieces of work had been plotting their wicked assassination plan for a very long time now. The house's full of written notes, graphs, schemes, timetables and itineraries, meeting schedules, all of which denote the ins and outs of the World President's Office."

At that moment, Brian was looking totally gobsmacked, dumbstruck, lifeless, staring at the horizon line.

"Oh, yes, and one last thing. Only a few minutes ago we captured two filthy young sluts just off the shore, striving to escape in a paddle boat. It turned out that their fingerprints were all around this place, so logically this indicates that they're accomplices as well. However, as you might expect, they weren't able to show any form of identification either."

Then Brenda and Alice were both pushed brutally toward the boys by two of the officers.

The General had also turned as white as a sheet by then.

"Don't you dare call us sluts, Mr. Brandon," Alice protested, seemingly flustered.

"Alice, don't even go there," suggested Brenda.

"No way, Brenda. I've really had enough of this nonsense," Alice turned toward the Minister again, "Look at me Vince. Can't you recognize my face at least; are you so useless? I'm the only one girlfriend Dixon's ever had. You despise me, coz you love Dixon as well, a bit too much in fact. You don't want any rivalry on the bedroom front, do you Vince?"

"Shut your slimy face, you dirty little witch or I'll do it myself, I swear." Vince turned crimson and took out his gun, firing a series of bullets in the air so as to warn Alice.

"Stop, stop, cease the fire, Mr. Brandon, please, I do beg you, sir," screamed the General in despair.

The next moment, everyone looked stunned. Alice

was lying on the ground, fighting for breath. There was a tiny streak of blood oozing from her forehead down her face.

Unfortunately, one of the bullets had ricocheted off the eaves of the concrete tile roof. The sound of the shattered tin was still reverberating like an ominous echo in Brian's ears. He ran up to Alice and lifted her head.

"Brian, please forgive me. We were given a mission, but we didn't mean any harm to you. We didn't know what Dixon had in mind." Tears mixed with blood were flowing down her rosy cheeks and slender neck.

"Alice, that wasn't your fault. I've already forgiven you. It's you who should forgive me for my rude manners. I like you so much now, after all we've been through together."

Alice attempted a smile, her face brightened, and her eyes sparkled with hope, looking intently at Brian. Then, suddenly, she stopped breathing.

Brian shuddered for a second, but then pressed his lips against hers to give her a kiss of life, shaking her shoulders and chest, desperately trying to wake her up, that is, to resuscitate her, if at all possible.

After a few minutes of unsuccessful attempts, Brian stopped and retreated helplessly, his tears rolling silently. Instinctively, he approached her face again and closed her motionless eyes. His face was now showing fury and desire for revenge. He stood up and turned toward the Minister.

"You killed her, Vince. You're a cold-blooded murderer; you don't deserve to live. I'll give it to you back sooner or later, don't forget," shouted Brian at the top of his voice.

"No Brian, *you've* just killed her. Guess whose words Dixon's gonna believe? Anyway, Alice was a lost cause that was searching for her own fatal end."

Brenda and Gary were distraught. They couldn't believe what they'd just seen and heard.

"Mr. Brandon, you should definitely be ashamed of your blatant negligence. Do I have to remind you that Alice was one of our top secret agents, very skillful and talented? What's more, she was in fact my niece and I won't forgive you that either," the General butted in, his eyes also damp.

"General, let me remind you who's in charge, first off. Secondly, if anyone of you here opens their mouth to speak about that, no matter what, I'll personally take care to shut it, just like Alice's dirty one, understand?" Vince waved his gun again menacingly.

"Mr. Brandon, I think we need to get in touch with the President immediately, for we have a serious situation here, don't you agree?" demanded the General.

"What for, General? What are you on about? To call the President? Why on earth should we? Just stop thinking," replied Vince sarcastically.

"Mr. Brandon, *we must* follow the procedures, is that correct?"

"Mind you, you're damn right, General. I'm gonna call President Sunderland this instant for I'm keen to sort this bastard Brian out at last. He really should get what he deserves." Vince's eyes widened with anticipation.

After a while, with the help of the officers, a video conference call with the President was set and ready to start. Prior to that, Alice's body was appropriately covered with a dark blanket.

The three suspects were briefed and advised to stay still and keep quiet during the whole forthcoming satellite call, unless further instructions were given or the President himself asked them to talk. Besides, by no means should they speak about Vince's random shooting. All of the above was done by the officers in a low-key but sufficiently clear manner.

[6]

BRIAN WAS A SORRY SIGHT, OF COURSE, BUT AN officer cared enough to wash his face a bit in order to look more presentable for the conference call with Washington, DC, where President Sunderland was currently residing.

"You want me to look better, officer, don't ya?" Brian tried to sound teasing.

"That was an order, so don't flatter yourself, boyo," the officer retorted harshly.

"Mr. Brandon, do you need anything else sir?" The officer turned to Vince.

"Thanks, my man, but I've got my beauty box with me wherever I go," Vince grinned, his teeth lustrous.

"What the heck, a beauty box, is this guy an aging fag or something? Perhaps poor Alice wasn't kidding at all," thought Brian to himself.

"I'll have to powder my nose and cheekbones for that little shit bruised and scratched my face quite badly. Or should I leave the scars just like that for the President to see what a naughty son-of-a-bitch we have in here? No, of course not. This would be rather disrespectful and—I'm a tough guy after all, right?"

"Yes, sir, that's absolutely right," a couple of officers recited almost automatically.

The General remained silent and thoughtful.

On the other hand, Brenda and Gary could hardly conceal their involuntary smirk, sitting on the ground by the helipad, handcuffed together, back-to-back.

"Did I say anything funny?" grumbled Vince, "I'll teach you how to show respect for authority, you two dumb lots."

"Minister Brandon, all the equipment is now poised, we've just received a confirmation from the President's administration that we can proceed, shall we, sir?" one of the officers raised his voice and spoke formally.

Vince, clearing his throat, looked in his pocket mirror one more time and answered:

"Yes, certainly we shall. We mustn't keep the President waiting. Let's get over and done with this mess, once and for all."

A few minutes later Dixon appeared on the wide 3D LED screen, mounted in front of the villa. The handcuffed suspects were huddling together, looking like a small cluster. Vince was in front of them, while the General was standing on the right. All of them were surrounded by the military officers.

"Good morning Mr. President," greeted Vince ingratiatingly.

"Hi guys, what have you got out there? Is everything alright?" Dixon inquired promptly.

"Well, hm, er, briefly, we caught the rascals on the spot as ordered, and now we're awaiting your further instructions sir. Shall we liquidate them straight away or what?"

"Wait, wait, my buddy, what are those reddish lines on your face, by the way, is that because of the video connection?"

"Actually, no, that's not the case. It was Brian, or the person saying he's called so, who violently resisted arrest, you see."

"Oh, I understand, so you are my hero then, Vince," jeered Dixon.

Vince got slightly embarrassed and kept quiet. Therefore, Dixon had to carry on: "OK, let's resolve this issue now, as soon as poss, so that I could have my dinner afterwards. Never mind, well done, Vince.

"Mind you, can I have a word with my sly little brother? Is that you Brian? Ain't you glad to see me? Why dontcha smile a bit? I can see Vince's given you a nice facelift—is that lipstick on your mouth, my li'l bro? Ha-ha." Dixon was laughing loudly and incessantly.

"No, Dixon. I, unlike you and your friends, have never used lipstick or makeup; those are the stains of my innocent dried blood you're so eager to shed hastily and recklessly. But first things first, you're well aware that this was an obvious setup, from start to finish, won't you admit? Despite all your malicious deeds, I've never ever intended to harm you in any way. I'm simply indifferent to you, you know that." Brian spoke with his broken teeth conspicuously showing. His face was ostensibly badly bruised and swollen.

"Listen to me very carefully, Brian. From now on, whatever you may think or say just won't matter in the slightest. You're already Mr. Nobody. You ain't my brother any longer. Your life isn't worth even a dime. Do you copy me?"

"Dixon, my big brother, what exactly do you want from me then? Why are

you doing this to me? I really don't get it, so please explain."

"I'm not the one to explain whatever. I'm the Master of the Earth; don't ever forget that. I'm the law across the world; I'm creating a whole new universe of mine and no one's gonna forestall my plans. And, finally, just stop calling me your brother, OK?" Dixon really meant it.

Apparently, he tended to get extremely irritated

every time he had to converse with his own little brother. Just like that, for no obvious reason.

"Alright Dixon, let's calm down a bit and—"

"No, you can't talk to me like that, you dunce. I'm the World President, simply accept that, stupid boy."

"Right, I understand, Mr. President," Brian uttered slowly to make a better impression.

"Now, you're talking; that's a lot better. Anyway, have you got anything else to say with your bloody mouth?"

"Sure, one final question if you'll allow me. So, are you gonna kill me after all, or what else do you wanna do with my life, Mr. President?"

"Ah, I see, you're learning fast, Brian, my little doggy. I think you'd actually wanna have died here and now, but there should be no mercy for you. You don't deserve any such kindness, you're such a worthless creature. From this day onwards, you're gonna be the world's most famous attraction, the monkey that wanted to assassinate the President. You're Terrorist Number One of all time. Even history's gonna remember you as such a notorious legend, an infamous character, an eternal persona non grata. However, your name will no longer be Brian. You'll have no human name; you aren't worthy of a name, you're just a number."

"Mr. President, may I add something here as well?" the General interrupted expediently.

"Hey General, what's up, old-timer? Don't worry, you'll be awarded great honors, medals and a wonderful pension scheme."

"Thank you, Mr. President, I do appreciate your kind gesture, but I was considering the issue of international human rights laws involved in the case at hand. Shouldn't we first of all consult the Governor of the Moon? Apart from this, Mr. Sunderland, Brian is or at least used to be your own brother—he might have to be granted the right to a last wish prior to his final verdict announcement and enforcement."

"Quite right, General, this yob WAS my brother, but now he isn't, 'cause he's a villain. Why are you so concerned about him, General, and why are you taking the side of such a most-wanted criminal then?"

The General froze, his hopes were crushed, turning into a pipe dream.

Dixon continued: "No, no last wishes for such baddies—that must be crystal clear. As for the ombudsman on the Moon, let me tell you something about him, General. He's an old bat, a prick with a demented mind. I wouldn't even bother if I were you."

The General kept standing upright, no facial muscles moving.

"But even if I agreed to send this trash to the Moon, then what? Should I call him a lunatic, or what? Besides, he might carry on committing serious crimes from there. Simply imagine him tampering with some confidential information, such as world digital records, including classified databases, military archives, personal files, etc. No way, General."

Dixon felt victorious and kept on verbally dooming his brother's life. "On the other hand, I can't let him be exiled to Mars, either. He'll undoubtedly instill his evil ideas into the other political prisoners on the red planet. Anyway, the only uplifting thought I might entertain would be that I should have to call him a Martian, you see."

"Dixon, really, why don't you kill me right now?" Brian suggested, determined to resolve the issue on the spot.

"Don't even mention that idea, Brian," the General said abruptly, his voice soft, low.

"Are you becoming friends with him now, General?" Dixon taunted with a snide smile. Then, he turned to Brian. "Alright, Brian—no, why the hell am I repeating this name, since such a person simply doesn't exist as per our records? You're basically erased from the face of the earth. Nonetheless, I'd love to see you suffering, you lowly worm."

"Why are you doing this to me, just tell me why?" Brian requested.

"You want to know the answer? Here it is, it's so damn simple—I've never liked you, anyway. You've repelled me since the day you were born. It's a real shame we had the same mother, because otherwise we've got nothing in common. Anyway, you'll no longer be my rival."

"Oh, Dixon, please, give me a break. I've always told you I've got no ambitions to rule or be in a position of power. Why don't you just let me go?"

"That's simply impossible; you aren't getting any further than the media coverage. You're gonna be in the spotlight, you'll be the center of attention, you'll be hitting the headlines, he-he. Your future home's gonna be the beast cell and your stage—the Grand Intergalactic Circus. You're already an attraction in chains. I've got big plans for you and your friends; you're on your way to stardom"

"My friends, what d'you mean? Please let Gary and Brenda go, they've got nothing to do with all that mess. You hate me, not them. They aren't related to you anyhow."

"No one's gonna be your friend anymore. The mere fact that they've been your friends at all makes them your accomplices. That's their own fault, period."

"Mr. Sunderland, what are you gonna do with me or us then?" Gary dared to ask.

"Is there an 'us' now, Gary? I was simply supposed to be your candy trap, remember?" mumbled Brenda under her breath.

"Ah, yes, Gary, your parents would be ashamed of you. Nevertheless, you shall live on Mars as a Martian, working hard from morning till night, building new homes for prisoners there together with Brenda, your new companion,

he-he. Did you have an exciting night, you two?"

"Dixon, Alice and I completed the mission as you ordered, so why should I be sent to Mars, if I may inquire?"

"Brenda, are you so naive indeed? Do you know how secret agents end up? Come on, you should be really grateful and embrace your new life, otherwise you'll be bound to die young and beautiful as it might've been like in your childhood dreams."

"You can't do this to them, Dixon. They're inno-cent," Brian jumped in.

"Can't I? Who says I can't? Should I remind you who's the Master of the World?"

"Mr. Sunderland, may I remind you that you need to consult the Moon Governor, Peter Fleming, about those verdicts first?" General Grant pleaded once again.

"Let your ancient friend on the Moon object, I don't mind, and can't care less. If he wants to oppose, he'll need to gather an army, which I seriously doubt, bearing in mind his very old age . . . his senility, that is."

The General finally resigned, caving in to Dixon's superior position.

"Anyway, I wonder why I can't see my sweet little orphan, Alice, whom you mentioned earlier; where's my dolly?"

Vince remained silent, presumably tongue-tied, while everyone else was staring at him inquisitively.

"Do I need to repeat myself," Dixon snapped. "What had happened? Was it you again Bri—you sod?"

"No, it wasn't me. You didn't deserve a girl like Al-ice," replied Brian, pouting.

"What was that supposed to mean? What are you talking about?"

"Actually, Vince killed her with his own gun, you may check for yourself if you want."

"Well, that's not exactly true; it was a terrible accident. I just wanted to warn the two little whor—ladies, I mean, Mr. President," Vince tried to defend and justify himself.

"Is that correct, General?" Dixon was now steaming.

"I can confirm that your younger brother Brian's telling the truth, sir," General Grant spoke in his typical matter-of-factly manner. "What's more, I sincerely hoped Alice was gonna change you for the better, but alas!"

"Stop bullshitting me, General. Cut this crap. I'm sure Brian's to blame for all that. As for Alice, if she's really dead now, who gives a damn? Who the heck was Alice? Anyway, show her to me this instant, that's an order!" Dixon screamed at the officers, seemingly aggravated.

They immediately stepped back and uncovered the blanket over Alice's dead body in a somewhat solemn way. Alice had been lying in the background since the start of the teleconference.

Dixon started zooming in on various minute details, examining Alice's corpse painstakingly. She still looked so young, delicate, but so—stiff, nonetheless.

"I demand all the audio and video files recorded by the CCTV cameras, all the footage there is, asap," Dixon uttered after a few minutes.

"Yes, certainly, sir," replied Vince quickly, his face pale. "Is there anything else I can do for you?"

"No," answered Dixon hastily. "I think that's really enough for now." He paused, scratching his head nervously. "On second thought, I might enjoy my little bro's performance for a couple of months, then throw him into jail for life or execute him publicly. That would serve as a warning to others. Commoners, I mean. Then, that'd be the last one of his gigs."

"So, Mr. President, are we dismissed then?" asked Vince, as he could bear no more suspense regarding his own fate.

"Sir, before we go, may I ask you a favor?" the General requested.

"Speak your mind fast," ordered Dixon.

"Thank you, Mr. President. Well, you see, Alice happened to be my niece, and only I know how much I'm gonna miss her, how deep my grief will indeed be at the end of the day." The General was beginning to get emotional.

"General, please spare me the sentimental bit and be brief; what is it exactly that you want?" Dixon seemed slightly more understanding now, but still as impassive as ever.

"Very well then, straight to the point, I agree. You know, I'm not able to return Alice back to life, no matter how much I want to, but what I can do is something else instead, with your kind permission, of course."

Dixon looked puzzled. "I hear you General, go on, don't waste my time," he urged.

"You know that Brenda was her best friend; after all, they were like sisters. Therefore, in commemoration of Alice, let me grant her and Gary special VIP status on Mars. I owe this to Alice at the very least. I have this privilege, which was given to me by you, Mr. Pesident, in accordance with the effective laws of the Solar Federation."

Dixon seemed absorbed in deep calculating thought. However, at that moment he was swift to respond. "General, who cares about laws, principles, duty, and honor nowadays? Anyway, if I give agree to that, then I'll be entitled to do whatever I want with my own prodigal brother.

"In addition, make sure the damn oldster on the Moon won't interfere, by any means. And there's one last condition, General; as you're aware, your privilege in question is to be used only once in a lifetime. Just like a one-off option, there's no way back, no return, so do we have a deal?"

"OK, Mr. President, yes, sure, I'd go along with that. At least I've tried my best. Do I have a choice, at all?" the General replied abruptly.

"No, you definitely don't, General. Mind you, I wonder who needs VIP status on Mars among those thugs, but as you like."

Then, Dixon spoke to Vince. "Now, Minister, it's high time we got this done: restrain my brother with a straitjacket, hand and foot cuffs, get him on board the chopper and fly off to Istanbul immediately. Then, you shall stay there until further notice.

"As for Brenda and Gary, make sure they fly to Cape Canaveral, Florida, so that they could catch the next flight to Mars, as I promised. You will escort them all the way to Florida, of course.

"I don't wanna see them anymore, as they remind me of Alice. I didn't think I'd miss her so much. Anyway, they should leave my planet as soon as possible. Needless to say, that has to be a one-way journey."

"Mr. President, how about Alice? Would you let me bury her where I deem appropriate?" the General asked.

"OK, just spare me the trivia, but where are you gonna do that?"

"In our family tomb in London, close to the War Memorial; she deserves that, sir."

"Alright, you have it, General, two wishes granted today. You can't really complain. Aren't I the goldfish for you then?"

"Well, Mr. President, there's one last thing, the third wish, so to speak," the General demanded, strangely jovial.

"What . . . more?" Dixon sounded a bit grumpy now.

"Well, Minister Brandon must be brought to justice, I mean to the Armed Forces Tribunal, no matter whether that was due to an act of gross negligence, abuse of power, or a pure accident."

"Don't you dare," Vince snapped, glaring at the General resentfully.

"Gentlemen, I consider the case closed now. Whatever there is, it's

between you two, I assume," Dixon interjected.

"I'll get back at you one day, Vince. I'll take revenge on you, never forget that—you'll never be forgiven," the General replied.

"Looking forward to that, General. Let's get even and sort this matter out soon, because I can't really wait," Vince hit back.

"OK, I'm off now then," Dixon cut their heated discussion short.

"Dixon, Dixon, just a moment please, may I?" Brian interrupted.

"Hey, freaky, what the heck do you want?" Dixon retorted in an ostensibly frustrated manner.

"Let me ask you only one question, just a small query, OK?"

"Alright, shoot then, dummy."

"Do you have any conscience at all, any common sense or feelings? Are you a monster or what?" blurted out Brian, shivering convulsively.

"Ha, who needs that, Brian? You're such a fool, so helpless and gullible. The only thing I like about you is actually your naivety . . . you're so easy to be taken in. You'd better relish your moment of glory, your fifteen minutes of fame, that is. Your time has come, boy. Farewell my li'l bro, I'm dying to watch your demise, he-he."

That second the connection was cut off. It started

to drizzle. Somewhere in the distance, a flash of lightning struck. Then, a moment later, a thunderbolt pierced the air. A gust of wind suddenly blew. The sky was heavily overcast.

Evidently, a violent storm was approaching, possibly a tempest.

They were forced to hurry up and lift off as quickly as possible. The Black Sea was unusually rough for this time of year.

[7]

THEY WERE FLYING SOUTH, VERY CLOSE TO THE seashore, only about a hundred feet above the water in order to dodge any radars and avoid any further troubles with their secret mission.

Brian was squeezed between two stocky officers, restrained and despondent.

Nearly three quarters of an hour into the bumpy ride and the cyclone had moved to the north, so the summer sun reappeared in the sky, just above the fleeting clouds, and shone brightly through the cockpit. The sea seemed calm and translucent. The helicopter's side windows were rolled down completely, as the weather was still hot and humid. Besides, the air-conditioning was not supposed to be used for the passengers' comfort. The military chopper was overloaded, having to carry a lot of luggage, passengers, and a dead body in the refrigeration cabinet, which seemed a bit small for that.

Suddenly, the pilot changed direction sharply in order to head east, away from the shore. Apparently, they were approaching the Bosphorus Strait. Some rocky cliffs and jagged stones like shards could be seen down in the shallow waters beneath them. That's why the water under the sea was not quite clear.

At that instant, while the chopper was maneuvering, Brian bent slightly forward, sneaked around for a second, escaping the two officers' tight clutch, and jumped out of the window, which was now facing downward, like a torpedo.

The two officers couldn't react appropriately because of the centrifugal force coupled with gravity. They were simply caught unprepared. Obviously, Brian had cleverly grasped the exact moment with an enviable sense of precision.

A few seconds later, they saw him plunge into the muddy waters of the treacherous sea. His movement was like a nosedive performed by a crashing plane. His flight was short and his splash quite noisy as the strait-jacket and chains weighed too much for his tallish and athletic but rather slim body.

When Brian's head hit the surface of the water, he felt extremely and inexplicably guilty, remorseful, desperate and useless.

Was Dixon right about his hopelessness then?

He went straight down to the seabed and it seemed as if he'd drowned immediately. The mass of seawater above turned red from his blood-soaked clothes that had previously dried.

For the previous hour or so, grave silence had ruled over the chopper. Only the rhythmic sound of the engine and the rotor blades was heard. Then, after witnessing Brian's unfortunate escape, Vince broke the tense silence with a holler, "Morons, you're so damn useless. How could you let him go so easily?" Vince was pointing at the two bulky officers at the back that had been sitting next to Brian, on each side, just a few moments earlier.

One of them tried to explain. "Well, Mr. Brandon, the chopper was slanting at a very sharp angle and we didn't realize he wanted to—"

"Just shut up, zip it, wankers," Vince interrupted,

obviously furious, but also quite worried. "Dixon wanted that bastard alive, but now what can we possibly do?"

"Mr. Brandon, let's turn back and search for Brian, shall we?" proposed the General.

"Turn back, huh? Do you realize we don't have any time for that now?" Vince continued to bark. "What else can we do?" He sounded desperate and scared.

Sensing that, the General urged, "We need to hurry, as he might've hurt himself against those sharp rocks down there, if not something even worse, God forbid! Besides, lately there've been some nasty little sharks seen swimming in these jinxed waters. That used to be so untypical some decades ago, really. Allegedly, they'd been artificially bred and introduced in here by the border authorities to avoid any illegal migration of people." The General's voice sounded seriously concerned.

Vince was still reluctant and of two minds but, without any further hesitation, ordered the pilot to turn back. He didn't want to upset Dixon further, bearing in mind the possible consequences for himself in case they couldn't manage to find Brian, dead or alive.

Several minutes later, Vince asked the pilot to lower the helicopter further and hover in mid-air. Using the ladder, and taking an inflatable boat with them, a couple of officers abseiled down to the bloody spot where they last saw Brian. They were just about to go snorkeling, when several sharks started to gather. They also used a thermographic camera, but again, without any success.

After about a quarter of an hour of futile search, Vince finally shouted over the Tannoy: "Haven't you found anything yet? Advise now?"

One of the officers spoke into his mouthpiece. "No, sir, there's absolutely nothing down here, only sea-weeds, underwater caves, rocks and swarming sharks, sorry. Should we abort the operation now and go back up?"

Vince turned livid. At that very moment, the pilot could see a coast guard boat in the distance. Upon hearing this piece of bad news, Vince replied, "No, stay there in the boat or sail to the coast. We've got no time now. We'll get in touch with you later; just try to hide somewhere, over and out."

Vince hung up and said to himself, "Unless you drown or get eaten by the sharks, you jerks."

Right then, numerous small sharks encircled the rubber boat and started biting it ferociously. Several seconds later, there was virtually no boat around the two officers, so they tried to swim to shore, but the beasts wouldn't let them go. Loud screams and cries were heard from down under. The water turned dark red.

"Move, move, off we go, fly away now! Let's get outta here," Vince ordered.

The pilot did as instructed. The chopper gained both altitude and velocity in no time.

The General's eyes were now wet. Gruesome, but deafening silence set in again.

Then, Vince rang up Dixon again from his smartphone, turning on its camera as well. "Hi, my hero, did you butt-dial me this time or what? Oh, I can see you're all packed like sardines inside the chopper. What's the matter?"

"No sir, I didn't pocket dial you. Unfortunately, we've got a situation here."

"What now? Can't you handle it on your own then? What's going on Vince? Don't tell me you've just messed up the mission of your lifetime?"

"Well, Mr. Sunderland, Brian, I mean, the prisoner committed suicide half an hour ago by cunningly sneaking out and diving into the shark-infested sea below. We then sent down two of our men to look for him, but they were also devoured by those bio-engineered beasts."

"Hold on, slow down, will you?"

"Yes sir, as you say."

"Tell me now, how can you be sure? I mean, did you actually see Brian's dead body and how can you state that the bastard's dead?" Dixon was boomed on the phone.

"Sir, we definitely saw the streaks of blood on the water's surface, trailing after he went undersea. As for the two officers, we could still see their bloody remains, namely pieces of ripped flesh, left over by the sharks, as well as their torn clothes floating around a few minutes after the accident. However, we had to fly away quickly, as the coast guards were approaching. Sir, I'm terribly sorry, I know you wanted the detainee alive, but we failed this time, we really screwed it up." Vince was sobbing.

"No, my man, you didn't, unless Brian is somehow miraculously still alive. Please confirm that he's gone. Otherwise, you should pray for your own life, Vince."

Vince didn't reply.

Therefore, the General butted in. "Sir, I can reassure you he was put into a straitjacket, his hands and feet were cuffed and chained. I doubt he could've survived anyhow. He'd definitely drowned, although we weren't able to find any trace of him."

"Amazing critters, aren't they, General? Nothing can virtually escape from their jaws. I should say, you two have just deprived me of my chance to see my little brother perform like a superstar, but that's fine. Seriously, he's much better this way . . . I mean dead rather than alive. However, if by any chance it turns out that he has survived, then both of you'll be held responsible, and I'll personally hold you liable for that, by all means."

"Yes, sir, understood," Vince replied eagerly and automatically.

"Yes, sir. But how about the other captives here, namely Gary and Brenda? Now that Brian's dead, should we still transport them to Istanbul or set them free?" the General asked.

"Set 'em *free*? No way. They're still criminals in my eyes, so they're bound to go to Mars and rot there sooner rather than later."

"I see, Mr. Brandon, but we have a deal with you, right? They'll be granted VIP status there, OK, sir?"

"Despite having such special status or privileges, they'll still be people of no importance among other criminals, prisoners and scumbags. The inhabitants there hate foreigners and will most likely kill 'em anyway. However, we do have a deal, General, I remember, that's right. I stand by my words."

"Yes, sir, I appreciate that, but in view of the latest developments and unforeseen circumstances, can't we repeal their cruel verdict and send them off to the International Space Station (ISS) at least? That's my kind request, Mr. President."

"General, I know where you're trying to lead us, but you certainly know the rules extremely well. The free movement of people, regarding journeys to Mars, the Moon, or the forthcoming Venus habitat is only one-way.

"Therefore, they'd better be sent to one of those destinations. Thus, if I allowed those rascals to go to the ISS on holiday, so to speak, and stay in the most luxurious hotels there, that'd be too risky, you see. Who knows, some crazy judge or an old jerk like the Governor of the Moon might appeal and even ask for their return to Earth later on.

"Then, in such case, I'd have no other choice but to execute them according to my own rules. You need to acknowledge that, General, I'm being honest with you.

Now, I can't look at their insolent faces any longer, so get them out of my sight at once," commanded Dixon.

"Dixon, do you love anyone else at all, apart from yourself? Essentially, you destroyed your own brother, your blood, your family, in fact. You're a tyrant, a psycho, you're pure evil. Be damned!" cursed Brenda.

"Shut up, you slut," Dixon growled.

"You entirely blew your chance to become a better person, Mr. President. Your brother and Alice actually loved you, but you wiped them both out by ruining their lives first," Gary answered back.

"Ugh, love, feelings, blah-blah-blah, you're so slushy and grotesque," Dixon retorted. "Vince, go now, and take those lots away from me; get them outta my face, and let's finally cut this farce. Will catch up with you later."

After Vince's short affirmative reply, the connection was terminated.

The chopper carried on flying without any change of direction. Deafening silence hung thick in the air again. Only the roaring sound of the blades was heard. There were tears rolling down the General's cheeks. Tears that had been held back previously.

Both Brenda and Gary seemed devastated but determined nonetheless.

"Brenda, I promise you, one day I'll avenge Alice and Brian, I will. Don't forget that, Vince!" cried Gary.

Vince went berserk, turned around, and punched Gary straight in the face. "Shut your face, dude," Vince replied. "Seal their mouths with a tape right now," he ordered.

The nearby officer did as instructed.

The helicopter was due to arrive in Istanbul in a few minutes.

$$[\ 8\ ]$$

During his sloppy plunge, hundreds of rebellious thoughts crossed his mind. He surely didn't want to die, let alone kill himself. He just wanted to escape, to wake up from this nightmare.

"Dixon seemed so powerful and arrogant, as if no one could ever put an end to his atrocities. He keeps ruining so many innocent lives, so many human destinies. He's an embodiment of monstrosity."

On the other hand, Brian had always believed his life wouldn't finish so abruptly and prematurely, at such a young age, in his prime. He had such wonderful plans for himself, for his best friend, for some other people on this poverty-stricken earth. He wanted to settle down, to start a family with a lovable girl, raise kids, feel loved. He'd felt like a destitute orphan ever since his mother's untimely death a few years back.

Splaaaaaaash!!!

Brian went underwater. He felt his head bump against a rugged cliff. He tried to move, but he couldn't budge an inch, despite being an excellent swimmer, due to the tightly fastened straitjacket and the cuffs that had badly injured both his wrists and ankles.

The caress of cool water felt so refreshing and pure on his face, however. The trouble was, he couldn't breathe at all now. Otherwise, the body of water above him didn't seem so deep and didn't even appear to be very far from the shore either.

"If only I could get rid of those chains, that bondage, this bloody burden. Damn you Dixon! How the hell did I deserve all that?"

While pondering his unlucky escape, his doomed destiny, Brian saw some scary sharks approaching. A moment later, he felt giddy, started losing consciousness, and nearly drowned.

"I'm dying after all. So, that's it, so sad! Goodbye life, bye big wide world. Farewell General, so long Brenda, see you later, Gary. Hi Alice, I'll be keeping you company soon, you won't be alone. Hi mom, I'm coming shortly . . . been missing you so badly."

As Brian was bidding his farewell to the world he'd known for the previous 25 odd years, suddenly, out of the blue, he felt something like an incredibly strong hand grabbing him firmly and then pulling him out of the water and away from his deathplace. He was moving extremely fast to somewhere else, not aware of where exactly though. He sensed the powerful motion of suction, a vortex, an invisible tunnel, a pipeline, or whatever.

Did it really matter?

He tried to open his eyes but wasn't able to.

"I'm losing my senses, I'm definitely dying. I hope there's another form of existence or a so-called afterlife, at least. Otherwise, I'd feel so sorry, for I couldn't save my current one. Who needs such a wretched life, anyway? My life sucked so much. But I'll do my best if I get a new lease of life, a new chance. I'm sure it's going to turn out fine then."

Brian wanted to weep, but there were no tears in his eyes.

Despite his young age and physique, his army training and skills, strong will and extraordinary intelligence, all his immense efforts to survive finally proved totally meaningless and futile. Brian looked like an innocent victim, a poor soul sacrificed for no good reason . . . as if he'd shot himself in the foot, as if he'd fallen into Dixon's trap, a wicked deathtrap.

All his vitality was vanishing irreversibly.

[9]

Dixon called Peter Fleming on the Moon right
after he'd received the latest update from the helicopter
about Brian's disappearance:

"Good morning, old thing," he greeted disrespect-
fully, attempting a sardonic smile.

"Good morning, Mr. Arrogant Bully. What made
you call me? How can I help?" replied Governor Peter
accordingly.

"Sorry to bother you during your eternal rest, Mr.
Fleming, but we had a minor accident in the Black Sea
region involving my obtuse or rather imbecile little
brother Brian and now we're notifying all local govern-
ments across the Solar System, including even the Space
Exploration Mission on Venus, which is still in its pilot
stage, in the pipeline, so to speak, apart from your do-
main, of course."

"Thanks for letting me know, Dixon, but how's your
brother Brian then?"

"Well, my Defense Minister and General Grant reported him dead, deceased, that is, and it looks like he's
so, indeed. However, I need to make sure that's true."

"And if that's so, will you be really happy, Mr. Nasty
Brother-Hater?"

"Look, 'Great-Grandfather' Peter, I didn't kill my brother, OK?"

"Listen to me very carefully, Dixon. I know exactly what you've been up to lately; don't ever forget I've got virtual access to all places on Earth, Mars, Venus, the ISS, the entire Solar System and beyond. The thing you did to your own brother was obnoxious, to say the least.

"I told you so many times before that I wanted your brother to help me up here. I even gave you my word that he'd never vie for your 'throne', but you paid no heed to my words at all, did you, Dixon?" Governor Peter sounded angry and distressed at the same time.

"Well, I see, gov'ner. In that case, let me tell you this one thing, old-timer. If you had wanted my unwanted brother so much, you should have fetched him yourself. But then you would have fought in combat against my army like a real man, without turning to your paranormal bullshit magic, your wishy-washy stuff, you know."

"Dixon, you should also know that I ain't afraid of you, but I wanted to ask why you hated your brother that much?"

"Oh, you're moralizing now, aren't you, poor thing? Please spare me this sentimental rubbish and listen to me too. You should understand that if, by any chance, Brian isn't dead and happens to be living somewhere else, apart from my Earth, I'll prosecute all his accomplices in the most severe way; is that clear, granddaddy?"

"Wow, I'm damn scared now. You'd better hope that your brother's still alive. As I told you before, the prophetic vision Lianne had was also confirmed by some of my old books here. And Dixon, remember: even if you destroyed your brother, you wouldn't be able to change the entire destiny for the worst, after all. Be it Brian, be it someone else, the good prophecy WILL come true and no one, including you, could ever stop or prevent it from happening."

"Right, I'm fed up with your blabbering, your make-believe, enough is enough. I warned you, oldster. That's all for now, old looney chap. And don't forget who's in charge now and forever."

"Dixon, rest assured that you aren't worthy of the throne and you ain't gonna rule over the world for too much longer now."

"That's that, I've really had enough! You pissed me off and I'm hanging up this very moment."

So, Dixon ended the call in a very rude manner.

10

SEVERAL YEARS LATER

"GOOD MORNING, MY SON," AN ELDERLY BUT RATHER energetic man greeted a younger one that was lying in bed.

The bed seemed to have been his usual if not constant abode for the past half dozen years or so. He appeared to be in his mid-thirties.

He was now desperately attempting to open his eyes, after hearing the greeting. It was extremely hard for him, as he hadn't done that in a very long time. After a while, he finally managed to blink a few times because the light was actually blinding him. Five minutes later, he was even able to make out the face of the elderly man that had greeted him.

"Ouch, aren't I dead?" the youngish man asked curiously, slurring his words, still suffering from dizziness and vertigo.

"Oh no, you ain't dead, far from it, hopefully. But that's good. I can see you still remember who you are, or were; that's a very good sign in itself," the elderly man responded obliquely, trying to make the younger guy relax.

"Who are you then, sir?"

"The question's not who I am, my son, but who *you* are, or who you *think* you are."

"Are you making fun of me?"

"No, not at all. Right, let's start from the very beginning. As far as I can see, you're in fairly good physical and mental states after all you've been through. My current name's Peter Fleming, but my surname used to be different long time ago. Anyway, as you might know, I'm the Governor of the Moon. Nice to meet you, young man." He paused to see how his interlocutor was taking in his words. The reaction wasn't delayed too much.

"Oh, so I'm on the Moon now? Never been there, I mean here, before. Anyway, what had happened to me, how did I get here, who found me?"

"Well, you're starting to ask too many questions. Hold on, we'll have enough time to discuss all your queries at length soon. But, first of all, you need to get physically fit enough before we continue further. However, along those lines, you know, Einstein said something like this: 'Logic will get you from A to B, experience can take you where you want, but imagination will take you everywhere.' Don't you think that's a genius thought?"

"Oh, science, right! Mind you, the last thing I remember is when I thought I was dying, or already dead, and then it all became a blur. Basically, nothing, blank, void. Was it my imagination? I dunno."

"Calm down, that's normal, for you were in a coma for quite some time."

"What do you mean? How long exactly? Oh God, so I WAS dead, more or les." The young-looking lad realized his circumstantial rudeness and tried to be a bit more polite.

"You see, Brian, I'm sure you remember your own name now, at least. Anyway, what I wanted to say was that in order to be really alive, you need to have been 'dead' first, if you know what I mean.

"Even babies, before they're born are not quite alive

yet, not according to most people, at least. Prior to being conceived, people are usually considered to be either unborn or non-existent, which is equal to being 'dead' somehow, right? It's a process of cyclic development, you see."

"I'm sorry, sir, I mean, Peter—was that your name?" interrupted Brian.

"Yes, that's correct. Go on Brian, speak your mind. Get it off your chest."

"Well, don't get me wrong, not that I wouldn't like some words of wisdom for the time being, as I deeply respect you and your rank, but I ain't in the mood for listening to some philosophical insights, at least not until I'm fully aware of my current situation. I think you do understand me," Brian rambled, partly reclining in a semi-recumbent position, trying to sit up as much as possible in his bed.

"Yes, Brian, I do very well in fact, 'cause I WAS in a similar situation many years ago. My name was effectively erased from the world records at the time. I was declared missing and, shortly after that, deceased. There was a war conflict on Earth, if you can remember, and I fought alongside General Grant and his older brother Philip—two of the most honored men."

"Wait! Are you talkin' about *the* General Grant and the late father of—Alice?"

"Yes, now you're talking mate. Did I finally manage to grab your attention? Mind you, I wanted to tell you about her mother, Teresa, too. She was also serving in the army then.

"Unfortunately, they were both killed in action, and Alice remained an orphan at a very young age. General Grant was her only living relative. He took good care of her, taking her under his wing, despite Gilbert Sunderland's dislike for their whole family.

"Afterwards, ironically, Dixon seemed to have fallen for Alice, so the General was quite happy and thought they might make up and forget about the feud, the longstanding rivalry and move on; I mean, the two families could've become closer."

"Yeah, I remember all those things, but no matter how hard I try, I'm still unable to remember you, sir, since you stated that you were so close to my family and friends. I guess you're aware of the fact that my granddad, Peter Drake, was the Commander-in-Chief of the World Defense Army?"

"Yes, my boy, I know that quite well indeed. By the way, who do you think Peter Fleming is, or rather *was*? That's me, I was, I mean, I AM your grandfather, Peter Drake, whom you could never possibly remember. Not because of your partial amnesia now, but coz I was officially pronounced dead just before you were born.

"Besides, I could no longer bear that surname; it would've been unthinkable, a real death sentence for me. Thereby, I took my wife's maiden name, that is, your granny Bridget's surname.

"No one knew her surname, not even my son-in-law Gilbert or his son Dixon, your evil brother, as it was top secret information, since she'd been recruited as a secret agent. However, I retained my family memories and kept my first name. I also completely changed my appearance for safety reasons, as you might guess."

"OK, I'd be really glad if my granddad were alive, but still, how can I be sure you're telling me the truth? Is that possible after all those years? And how old are you supposed to be now? Somehow you don't look so—"

"Right, I should give you the benefit of the doubt, Brian. You may take your time. As for my age, ha-ha, you wanna know how old I am, yeah? Well, I'm pretty old, but nevertheless, I consider myself to be in my golden years, my prime, my heyday, you see."

"I should admit, I wish I could look like you at your

age indeed," Brian replied in a slightly friendlier way this time.

Sensing that, Peter continued. "However, there's one thing you need to promise me now, Brian. That should be our best-kept secret. You mustn't tell anyone who I actually am, not that anyone would believe you anyway, but bearing in mind how much my ex-son-in-law Gilbert and his son Dixon used to despise me, I can't risk giving myself away, you know. Dixon is a chip off the old block."

"Ah, of course I do. I promise, you have my word; we're both in the same boat, you see. Like grandfather, like grandson, kinda, Governor Fleming. Anyway, thanks for saving my wretched life. The way you did it, however, still remains a bit of a mystery to me, but by all means, I'm extremely glad to be alive. I'm over the Moon, in fact. Perhaps I should've told you these words the minute I opened my eyes, but I was still in a state of shock, sorry." Brian even attempted a smile, but then suddenly winced and looked startled, even embarrassed.

Peter encouraged him, as if he were reading his mind, "Don't worry about such trivial things anymore, Brian; you don't need to. Your smile is again bright and handsome, unlike before."

Then, Peter took out a pocket mirror and handed it to Brian to have a look for himself. He thought Brian should be ready for that by then—that is, for the moment of truth.

So, Brian looked in the mirror and seemed perplexed, to say the least. "But how's that possible? Is this me?" He could hardly recognize himself.

"Well, it's definitely not me, my son. What's the problem? You're still much younger than me, though a bit wiser and more respectable, I guess. You've gained a few pounds and your muscles are visibly tighter and bigger, 'cause you were taken good care of."

"Oh, I see. So did you look after me while I was unconscious and, by the way, how long did it last overall?" Brian questioned.

"A-ha, well, talking about time, you should know that it's also relative as Einstein suggested many years ago.

"In terms of our Solar System, it's dependent on the rotational and orbital speed of each planet and its distance from the Sun. As you might guess, for example, Mars and the Moon have very different rotational and orbital speeds from those of Earth.

"Basically, the paradox states that the faster you move or travel, the longer you live and vice versa. But, otherwise, it's not so simple and straightforward. It's again case-wise. Generally, people adjust and react to the different time zones differently.

"By the same token, life as such is different on different planets. However, on average, nowadays people living on the Moon or on Mars tend to live longer, as they usually lead a healthier life. Hence, they look much younger. Overall, longevity is the norm in such newly colonized habitats."

"Fair enough, but just out of curiosity, how do you define the exact date and time on a daily basis, especially in terms of business? Do you have a unified standard or benchmark?"

"Yes, you're on the right track my son, exactly. We officially follow, or rather take account of, the Earth's time zones and calendar, for convenience purposes. That's done mainly in order to avoid chaos or disorder.

"Nevertheless, we have our local times and cycles on the Moon, as we can also see the Sun, when there's day or night.

"Of course, there are some wicked circles that would gladly wreak havoc with that issue, if allowed. You see, the balance is quite fragile, and we need to protect it diligently." Peter was about to wrap up his mini lecture when he realized he had to share something far more important. "Oh, at the end of the day, you should be really grateful to Tom and Donna Starling for the care they took of you while on the ISS. Luckily, Dixon couldn't realize you were there and who you actually were. You already looked so much different at the time.

"You'd already changed beyond recognition by then, that is, as a result of the concussion you'd suffered after banging your head against the rock that fortunately resembled a boulder rather than a shard.

"Luckily, in a way, water had softened the hit. Also, you should thank John, my private pilot, for he found you just in time. He literally saved you and, thank goodness, nobody saw him, as he was using some stealth technology to hide his spacecraft-cum-aircraft."

11

"So, your pilot John had saved my miserable life then, is that right?" Brian wanted to confirm.

"Yes, we all wanted you to survive, Brian. You were given a second chance, so to speak. Wasn't that what you'd been asking for? You weren't gonna kill yourself, were you?"

"Well, I ain't suicidal at all, to begin with. But, how do you read my mind, Peter? Are you sure you're the one you say you are? Are you actually a living person or something more?" Brian was bewildered again.

"Look Brian, let me explain. Here, on the Moon, we keep all the knowledge and wisdom of the world, or the Solar System rather, if not the entire Galaxy, or the Universe."

"Now, that was a metaphor, or an overstatement, right?" Brian exclaimed.

"You need to decide for yourself, Brian, but what I meant was that we're actually more technologically advanced than Dixon's army of human 'robots' and villains."

"But you ain't really telling me you've got an army, are you, my old granddad?" Brian jeered.

"I don't blame ya, my son. Maybe you think I'm an

old crook or something, but in fact I do have an army, although not as ordinary or visible."

"Then, why don't you overpower Dixon and put an end to that whole damn thing, the bloody agony I mean, once and for all? You know he's responsible for Alice's death as well as many other despicable deeds."

"Well, Brian, you hit the nail on the head now. Actually, we've been waiting for you to come up and vanquish Dixon's army. OK, let's get serious now. First off, we need to be much better than Dixon, you see. In fact, defeating Dixon definitely won't bring peace to our world. His close friends would seek revenge afterwards. Violence brings violence, after all."

"And how are we gonna win this battle then? Have you got an idea, Sage, or should I call you a buff?" Brian got shirty and disheartened at the same time.

"So, it's us now; that sounds more agreeable. Anyway, when the time's right. In other words, we need to bide our time—that's the recipe, basically. Usually, you can't be ahead of time, it makes little sense. Normally, time moves forward and not backward, it's as simple as that.

"However, some evil whisperers desperately want to stop it from advancing by any means possible, mostly by misleading other people and depriving them of their hopes. Ironically, it's relentlessly ticking away for them."

"OK, got it. What could I possibly do to help? Obviously, I shouldn't go back to Earth now that I'm here on the Moon with you, after such an ordeal. Moreover, it's against some of the laws that were introduced by Dixon's administration."

"Not quite. For example, let's take John, who holds all types of pilot's licenses and astronaut certificates. Pilots and astronauts can go back and forth across planets, outer space, space stations and suchlike. They're the only ones that travel around without any unnecessary hassle."

"But as far as I know, generally, it's extremely hard to get either an astronaut certificate or pilot license nowadays, irrespective of the type, be it private, commercial, transport and so on," objected Brian.

———

"Well, I haven't said it's easy. Mind you, at the ISS they completely regenerated your cells, rejuvenating your whole body in a natural way. Tom and Donna have worked miracles on you there. I'm extremely proud of them and their beautiful niece."

"And who's their niece, then?" Brian inadvertently brightened up.

"Ah, now you're talking, young man. I'll introduce you later. But again, it's a secret. Dixon doesn't know she's their niece. She was also an orphan. I'm like a father to her, as they entrusted her to me, and she's lived under my protection ever since."

"But Peter, how come Dixon doesn't have a clue who you are? That simply doesn't make any sense, since he's far from being stupid, quite clever and cunning in fact, never mind being evil."

"You're right, my boy, he's very clever indeed. However, Peter Drake's officially dead according to the records. Despite the fact that there are no DNA samples of Mr. Drake available, I had to edit, that is, modify my DNA a bit, just to be on the safe side. Do you follow me, Brian?" Peter wanted to make sure Brian wasn't bored to death by his story.

"Besides, when I stepped into office on the Moon, Dixon was still a little boy. Anyway, the council of elders elected me unanimously. That was soon after they'd found me literally dying on the battlefield, amongst other soldiers in the Rebel Army, which was fighting against Gilbert's forces."

"I could picture that. And what about their niece; is she as beautiful as you say she is?"

"Oh, I see, even more than that, I can assure you. Nevertheless, first of all, don't you wanna know anything about your best friend Gary and his beloved wife Brenda, the present governors of Mars?" Peter urged.

"Of course, Gary, yes, certainly, please tell me more. I'm so happy for him, I mean, them," Brian felt ashamed that he hadn't asked about him earlier.

Sensing that, Peter continued his account in a reassuring tone. "No need to feel embarrassed, Brian. You're still experiencing the aftereffects of a great shock, and that's quite normal. These are post-traumatic signs that will eventually disappear, without any further relapses."

"Thanks Peter, it's good to know. I ain't delusional, at least. Anyway, so Gary and Brenda, huh, well done, that's incredible. But how did Dixon let them do that? They were both prisoners, banished to Mars for life like me, right?"

"My son, you spent several long years in a state of profound coma. You

see, in the meantime, some things have changed for the better.

"Certainly, Dixon vigorously opposed those changes all the way. However, after holding a plenary session of the inter-planetary council at the ISS, the 2,500 senators, representing the Earth and all its space territories and colonies, voted in favor of Mars's independence. In other words, something similar to the Moon's autonomy.

"Hence, they elected their own local government, together with governors and a senate. A referendum had also been held there beforehand." Peter paused for a few seconds, taking a few deep breaths. Then, he continued cautiously, trying not to sound mawkish. "Apparently, Gary and Brenda were regarded as the most respectable, presentable, highly educated, still young etc. And, last but not least, having been granted VIP status previously, they proved to be so people-friendly and charismatic that all Martians loved them very much."

"So, has Dixon been furious ever since?"

"Very much so. Since then, he's kept calling me various names like old prat, geezer and git, as you might guess. You see, he used to think all his wicked plans had been set in stone and no one could ever disrupt them, but apparently that wasn't the case anymore."

"I see, and what about Gary's parents—how are they? Do they miss him a lot now?"

"Hm, er, yes, they were also happy to see their son become a governor a few years ago. Unfortunately, they both passed away about six months ago. Dixon made their life a misery by not letting them fly to Mars to see their only son again. Sorry, Brian, but I couldn't spare you the truth now." Peter was deeply saddened.

"Damn Dixon, he's a real monster." Brian started cussing.

[12]
SEVERAL HOURS LATER

"Now, let's get you out of this bed at last and see if you're still able to walk before you could learn to fly. I want you to meet someone that's very close to my heart," Peter told Brian, his eyes sparkling.

Brian felt much better; his life was meaningful again. Somebody needed him, but what for? He wasn't quite sure yet. Moreover, he was already sick and tired of asking the dumbest questions, notwithstanding his current delicacy and vulnerability.

"I see you haven't forgotten how to walk. Your legs still serve you quite well," encouraged Peter in a jovial way, while helping Brian stand up and take his first steps in a long time.

Brian was still feeling rather weak, feeble and frail, but walking seemed to be less difficult than he'd imagined.

"I guess it's more of an instinct than willpower for the time being. I feel as if I'm riding a bike again. You never forget such skills, do you? We're like grown-up kids after all, yeah?" Brian cheered up.

Peter seemed content with the rate of Brian's physiological recovery.

"So, are you ready to meet Lianne then, young man?" asked Peter solemnly.

"Oh, isn't it a bit too early for that? I still walk like an old-age pensioner and besides, why do you want me to meet a gorgeous young lady right now? Just look at me; simply put, I'm a wreck." Brian looked hesitant and his previous confidence disappeared.

"Well, compared to the time when you were in a coma, I wouldn't say you're a wreck now. Honestly, if only I could be a wreck like you, ha-ha! Anyway, don't flatter yourself too much.

"But take it easy as that might be a very good sign—apparently you're getting back to your past levels of self-consciousness and self-esteem, regaining your usual vanity, for better or worse.

"However, I just wanted her to keep you company while you're still on the rebound, you see. What else did you think, naughty boy?" Peter sounded ambiguous, but was attempting to look supportive.

"Oh, sorry, I see, my mind's still boggling, and I feel a bit lost, in fact. Of course, I see that I ain't so young and good-looking anymore. I still wonder why you saved me in the first place. Wouldn't it be much easier now if you hadn't brought me back to life? At the end of the day, why did you take such pains to resuscitate me?"

"Brian, you'd better have a break now. Some respite will do you good indeed. Let's bide our time. You don't need to get too emotional; you must spare your energy. However, you should socialize in order not to feel lonely among the old people around here on this little natural satellite."

Then, Peter asked John to call for Lianne.

About a quarter of an hour later John returned and demanded that the two gentlemen exit the room and follow him into the garden area, which at that time of day had a magnificent view of the setting sun.

Peter tried to prop Brian up a bit, but he was too proud to let him do that and refused, for he wanted to look manly enough. Somehow, nonetheless, he managed to sport an upright posture while attempting to walk smoothly.

"Hello, old guys," greeted a shining young lady, her wavy fair hair falling gracefully upon her shoulders. Her eyes sparkled emerald.

Brian was bedazzled by her smile. "Nice to meet you, Lady Lianne." He grabbed her slender hand and kissed it gently.

"I was gonna introduce you to each other, but that seems already redundant. I can't believe Brian looked so reticent just a minute ago.

"Anyway, I've gotta get back to my office now, my kids. You may sit down there on the garden bench and have a chat for a while before dinner. Enjoy each other's company." Peter showered them with his awkward matchmaking talk while making toward the exit. Then, he was gone in an instant. So, the two young souls were all alone.

The sunset was so brilliant at that moment. Brian displayed deep amazement. Lianne stood between him and the sun. Her hair was pure reddish-gold, sun-kissed, and radiant. Her face was beaming with joy.

13

"UNCLE PETER'S BEEN TELLING ME SO MUCH ABOUT you, Brian. I'm glad you can already walk so well. How do you feel? Still on the mend?" Lianne chirped like a nightingale.

"Ah, yes, I'm fine, very well in fact, thank you, Lianne. And why do you call him 'uncle'? I thought you weren't related in any way," asked Brian, curious.

He was willing to talk to her for hours on end but, at the same time, was not quite sure how to start, for fear of boring her.

"No, of course not, he's like a father to me, as I lost mine a long time ago."

Brian knew the answer, of course, but was striving to keep the conversation going with the most impressive lady in the universe.

Suddenly, the tiny little place called the Moon seemed so awe-inspiring and delightful to Brian. He felt young and strong again, uplifted and optimistic, brimming with hope, full of dreams and reveries.

"And so, what is a great lady like you is doing in this gloomy old place?" Brian finally dared to ask.

Then he blushed, thinking what an idiot he might seem to her.

"Thanks for the compliment, Brian. But why are

you asking me this question, aren't you a bit too old for me? You could well be my uncle too, right?" Lianne joked in a light-hearted manner, effectively breaking the ice between them, so delicately and, at the same time, so powerfully.

She was conversing with him so effortlessly and innocently that Brian was both impressed and bemused. She looked breathtakingly beautiful, whereas her mind was incredibly sharp for her young age. Wise words were coming out of her mouth. Eventually, Brian started to feel more and more at ease in this extraordinary girl's company.

"Has Peter discussed with you anything about your future plans, missions and perspectives yet?" Lianne asked openly and sincerely.

"Well, you got me there. I just woke up this morning, you see, and we spoke about some rather insignificant matters." Brian was desperately trying to appear intelligent and serious.

"I see, so you haven't got a clue why he wanted you here in the first place, admit it Brian," Lianne teased.

Brian simply shrugged his shoulders. Lianne laughed contagiously and disarmingly.

He felt hopelessly attracted to this lady, who he'd met only minutes earlier. He was really smitten, lovestruck, even besotted with her, something quite unusual for him—up until then.

"Perhaps I'm not the right person to tell you this, but he hopes you're the one who could overturn Dixon's lawless rule and change our world for the better soon."

"No way, look at me, I've been such a loser, a damn nutter, so far, you see. Dixon even dubbed me an impostor once. I've got no experience of warfare, let alone governance of any kind. He must've been joking. However, I'm extremely grateful he saved my poor life and thus I actually met you."

"Don't underestimate Peter's assessment skills. I wonder what name Peter's gonna come up with for you from now on. However, I hope I haven't given you a false impression, Brian—we could just be friends for now. Besides, you are definitely not my type, old sport."

"Yeah, you're right Lianne, as ever. I was just gonna ask Peter about my new name, since it'll be unthinkable to bear my old one for the time being."

Brian wasn't certain if Lianne was kidding again, but he wished she wasn't.

"It's time for dinner, sweethearts. Please come and join us in the large dining room," John called to them from inside the adjacent biome, where the governor's residence was.

Brian felt slightly disappointed by how fast the time spent with Lianne had elapsed. On the other hand, what exactly was he after? What did he want? It wasn't too much, was it, after all?

Probably, he simply had to be grateful for being alive and keep it that way, nothing more. Who was he, and did he deserve anything more? Those were the unsettling questions that kept troubling his mind.

14

TWO WEEKS LATER

"So, is everything ready for our battle against the Moon, Vince?" demanded Dixon.

"Yes, sir, we're all set and ready," replied Vince quickly, "but let me check on the General's unit too."

"Why do you always have to double-check with the General, Vince? Who's the Master here? Anyway, ask the General to come here, now," Dixon hissed.

They called for the General straight away.

"So, General, are you with or against me? I know about your old friendship with Peter Fleming, the old crook."

"Mr. President, do you really have any irrefutable evidence that Mr. Fleming is guilty of all those allegations, that is, of the so-called pre-planned uprising?

"And, besides, you need to communicate your intentions to him; you have to let him know, that's the law. We definitely don't need another bloodshed within the Solar System, do we?

"We've already had enough of such bloody conflicts so far, don't you think so? I kindly ask you to reconsider that decision and seek any other ways of resolving the issue, by diplomatic means maybe.

"Moreover, we aren't sure which side Mars will take, if and when they hear about your secret plans."

"Don't ever think of a mutiny, or an insurgency to that matter, General. That's the last time I'm warning you."

"As we're all agreed, we need to act fast now," Vince interrupted.

"Please, be quiet, Vince," the President ordered, then continued addressing the General. "Mr. Grant, I'm sure Brian's alive and well, residing on the Moon with the worst traitor of all time, the despicable snake Peter Drake, aka Fleming. Did you really think I wouldn't ever find out?

"Anyway, according to our rules, they all have to die, as they rightly deserve. As for the Martians, Gary Scholes and Brenda Collins, they're already personae non gratae for me.

"Not only were they accomplices, but you also granted them VIP status and, somehow, the ancient Peter managed to convince the Universal Assembly to promote them to governors there while still in exile—something unheard of.

"However, I'll never leave those criminals alone. I can't allow this any longer. But I will definitely sort out the Moon first. So, once again, are you staying with me, General, or do you want to follow their hapless fate, the fate of their parents and all other rebels?"

"Sir, may I remind you that you could still change your mind. Please, I'm begging you, indeed. Otherwise, I'll continue to serve you as I served your father and his father, Mr. Drake, your granddad, of course. But at the end of the day, Brian's your only brother. He hasn't done anything wrong, sir."

"No, General, he's certainly to blame, together with the old bastard Drake. Brian's an impostor and he most likely believes the prophetic rubbish the so-called oracle's told him . . . what was her freaking name? Yeah, Lianne the bitch, the damn whore."

"Sir, what about the ISS? Since we're bound to go

past it, it'll be too risky. They might well detect our spaceship and find out about our mission."

"Are you really that stupid, General? Tom and Donna Starling, the old couple, are so useless that they couldn't possibly be an obstacle for me and my legendary army. And just look at that sod, Drake; has he got an army at all? Maybe a handful of retirees, pathetic zombies, and frail swots, ha-ha." Dixon started laughing.

Vince joined in, unaware of how bizarre the scene was.

"Sir, aren't you afraid of retribution? The road you're taking is leading to perdition; it's a deadly route," the General pleaded.

"Afraid? Who me? No, of whom? Of destiny or the poor old bats? No way. Who can possibly stop me? I'm the sole Master of the Solar System, and soon of the Galaxy perhaps, or the whole Universe, he-he."

"Dixon, you could still go back and reconsider your course of action. You can learn to love, work together with other people, liaise with the various local governors, even your brother," the General admonished.

"Stop blabbering, General. You're being too emotional, which overshadows your sound reasoning. But remember General: emotions, especially regret, are only for the weak and the foolish. No one needs such rubbish."

[15]

AFTER DINNER, THE GOVERNOR HAD A WORD WITH Brian. "So, how are you feeling now, young lad? Your body's not gonna betray you soon, like mine, right?"

"Well, thanks for asking. I seem to be recovering much faster than I expected. Mind you, you appear to be in pretty good shape yourself too, old chap," replied Brian.

"You know, mind's much more powerful than matter. Let me show you something." Then, Peter sat by the side of a small pond, concentrating on a statue of a baby angel with a pebble in the centre. Several seconds later, Brian saw the pebble turn red, melt, and burst into flames. Then, it exploded like a tiny firework. The accompanying sound was reminiscent of heated popcorn.

Brian was deeply impressed. He thought that was unimaginable.

Overwhelmed with reverence, he exclaimed, "And how exactly did you manage to do that, Mr. Governor?"

"That was a little magic, my boy," Peter beamed with contentment. "You can also do that."

"Really? Do you mean right here, right now? Is that because we're on the Moon?"

"Don't be so daft, Brian. Be it on the Moon, Mars or Earth, the laws of physics hold true all around. I mean, under the Sun, at least.

"It's because you're a good mensch and, last but not least, you're my grandson. However, you still need to develop your potential and acquire the skills to control the elements for the sake of humanity. Unlike Dixon and his late father."

"Are you saying that Dixon has such powers too?"

"Well, not as great as mine, but he's quite clever and —evil, unfortunately. But anyway, don't tell me you've never experienced or sensed your potential powers?" Peter's eyebrows rose with surprise.

Brian cringed, not knowing what to say. Those things seemed really convoluted to him.

"Never mind, such powers are worthless without an honest heart, without love and empathy," Peter assured Brian, breaking the awkward silence. "And speaking of love, how do you find your new friend, Lianne?" Peter changed the subject with that cheeky question, gently poking Brian in the elbow.

Brian hesitated again, but since he had so many unanswered questions, he finally opened his mouth. "Honestly, Peter, I don't think she was impressed with me at all. Just have a look at me—I'm Mr. Nobody, who was saved by you. And my life's a total mess, you know."

"So, does that mean you're interested in her opinion of you after all?" teased Peter.

"What d'you mean? That sounds like a helluva leading question, an interrogation in fact. Does that matter at all? She mentioned something about a mission we, I mean, I should accept; what the hell's that all about?

"And what's a stunning Princess Lianne doing on this freaking Moon? Excuse my obscene allusions, Peter, but can't you see my point?"

"I can hear you guys. What are you discussing so eagerly?" Lianne's voice pierced the air from the hallway.

"Ah, Lianne, you're back. We were just discussing how Brian's recovery was going," answered Peter immediately.

Brian's face was bright red.

Lianne simply smiled and continued, "Uncle Pete, it's urgent. I came back coz I felt that time's running out and we need to act, react, or proact accordingly. Did your agents deliver the latest news from Earth? How are things there?"

"Yes, love, that's exactly what I wanted to speak to you about. Glad you're here now, my dear child."

"What are you two talking about then?" Brian asked, perplexed. "Planet Earth, secret agents, what's going on there? Is Dixon still around, that damn psychopath. What's he up to? I'd almost forgotten about him."

"Unfortunately, your so-called brother knows that you're alive and is heading toward the Moon, as we speak," Peter explained quickly.

"Oh gosh, blimey, crikey! So why are we still sitting like this? What are we gonna do about it? Can I help somehow?" Brian was nervous and excited at the same time.

"Yes Brian, you certainly can. Come with us. We must board the space shuttle this instant. John's already waiting for us there. Thank goodness everything's within easy reach around here," Peter replied.

"Yeah, right, everything's within walking distance indeed and it's quite hard not to feel claustrophobic," Brian jeered.

"Whatever, there's really no time to waste. So, we have to act fast, but wisely as well. Let's go!"

"But Granddad Peter, you don't really have an army, and as far as I can see, you've got only one spacecraft, which could serve as a space fighter. However, compared to Dixon's fleet of military spaceships and shuttles you just—"

"Uncle Pete has much more than that, Brian, take it easy," interrupted Lianne.

"With all due respect, Lianne, ain't I supposed to face my own brother myself and sort out this whole mess? In fact, I was the one that got you into trouble. And besides, you haven't answered my question yet, which was, I wonder why you saved my a—er, my soul in the first place?"

"Glad you didn't say anything inappropriate at least, Brian, but in the future, please mind your language in the presence of a real lady," Peter scolded.

"Alright, sorry, but do you have a plan at all?"

"Yes, I do, Brian, for your information. Also, if you wanna be a dead hero, just go ahead and sacrifice your life. You'll do Dixon a favor then. He'll be so happy, together with his bunch of wicked goons."

"No, I definitely don't wanna do that. I meant no disrespect to you, please accept my sincere apologies. I'm grateful to you and will do as you wish. I'll listen to you carefully and obey, no more stupid questions, I promise," Brian sounded much more relaxed and ready to cooperate.

Shortly afterwards, all three of them boarded the shuttle and it started taking off. They could see what was going on around Planet Earth and, in particular, Dixon's spaceship upon the screen, rapidly advancing toward them in a menacing way.

It was a scary sight to watch and things weren't looking good. They were even able to hear what Dixon and his lapdog Vince intended to do to the good old Moon.

Their spaceship was enormous and frightening in comparison to John's tiny little shuttle, which looked more like a tin can, whose only advantage, if any, was its super maneuverability, which was likened to the agility of a wildcat.

However, it wasn't at all certain if it could fly fast enough to escape in the worst-case scenario. More or less, they seemed doomed. They only hoped that the worst wouldn't come to the worst.

"ARE THE MISSILES READY, VINCE?' INQUIRED DIXON.

"Affirmative sir," reported Vince.

"Great. In a minute, I'd like to flail those zany lots with vast pleasure. Just wait for my command," instructed Dixon and then turned toward Mr. Grant. "And you, General, you'd better keep quiet and carry out my orders, for I don't wanna listen to your unfounded apprehensions and rubbish common sense like your sclerotic friend on the Moon, right?"

The General remained silent, as instructed, his face rigid and tense.

Suddenly, a voice blasted through the spaceship loudspeakers: "This is the ISS Space Guard Center speaking. Do you copy us? You're breaching our airspace. Answer immediately or, otherwise, we are entitled to take all necessary steps to stop you."

"How did they manage to detect us, General?" Vince asked derisively.

"I've got absolutely no idea, Minister. In fact, it was your techies that had equipped this spaceship with all the latest gadgets and gizmos," he replied aloofly.

"Let me answer them, Vince," Dixon demanded.

Vince handed him the microphone and put him through to the ISS space guards.

"President Dixon here. I hear you loud and clear. Please stay away, let me just pass by your station, and you're gonna be fine.

"Otherwise, I'll have to blow the entire ISS station up with my powerful weapons. Do you roger that? Besides, you don't have any military power to prevent my spaceship from proceeding further. No one can thwart my plans.

"So, I'm above the law and I myself represent the supreme, the ultimate power over the whole Solar System, and I could do whatever I deem proper, so beat it; understand?" snarled Dixon.

"OK, Mr. President, you could've notified us of your intended journey, at least," the ISS guard commented coolly.

"Just don't tell me what I should've done! It was supposed to be a top-secret mission, but apparently there are too many traitors at every corner.

"Now, I'll ask you one more thing. Listen carefully—don't report any part of our conversation to anyone or else you shall bear the most severe consequences."

"With all due respect, Mr. President, I can't see a reason why other governors won't be able to detect you, as we did. Anyway, bon voyage; have a safe trip."

Dixon grew impatient. His iniquity didn't allow him to wait any longer. He screamed, "Take aim at the Moon and fire now. Don't delay the attack. Act now; that's an order, morons!"

"Wait, stop right where you are! Can you all hear me?" Peter's voice suddenly pierced through Dixon's flight deck.

"Oh, Peter, is that you, my old looney traitor?" replied Dixon with another question.

"Dixon, my son, what do you think you're doing? Cease fire; this insanity must stop at once. You can't destroy the Moon alone. You'll surely knock the whole

Solar System off balance, thus bringing about an apocalypse."

"So, who's gonna stand in my way then? You or my little bro, Brat Brian?" Dixon gloated over their apparent position of inferiority.

"Dixon, my brother, I'm prepared to die for these people who saved my life. Just take my life, but let them live. All that objectionable nonsense should end, don't you think so?" Brian's voice could now be heard and he popped up on the screen right next to Peter.

"Yes, Brian, I'll be more than happy to end your pathetic existence. However, I wonder if you really wanna sacrifice yourself for others, or you just wanna be a damn superhero," Dixon replied with a smug smile. "You're a dead man already, my bro; you're doomed to eternal oblivion."

"Dixon, even if you exterminate your own brother, somebody else will come 'round, and save us from your turpitude," Peter advised solemnly.

"I'm telling you for the umpteenth time to cut your gibberish," Dixon retorted.

"Mr. President, I'm sure we could resolve this issue in a peaceful and diplomatic way. And besides, why do you hate your brother so much? Don't you love anyone in this world, apart from yourself?" Lianne asked.

"That's really enough now. You're all so small, insignificant, and ridiculous. There's no such thing like love. Who needs that at all? Power's the only measure of happiness and success. Naturally, I have it in abundance."

"Only for the time being, Dixon. You keep breaking the laws of the universe and that certainly can't go on forever. You realize that, don't you?" Peter asked with a scowl.

"Once again, and that'll be the last time, I promise —I won't discuss this matter with you. Just say your farewells to this world and go to hell; you don't deserve to live any longer," Dixon screamed.

"Before you proceed any further, I can't possibly let you carry on committing such unheard atrocities. No way, you know. You ain't God," Peter warned, his tone and expression grave.

"Hey, sclerotic oldster, what's wrong with you? You're wasting my precious time. I've got great deeds to perform, to write the new world history, and you're trying to stand in my way, you dunces!

"Can't you understand that you'll be gone in a minute, even in a few seconds, the moment I press this button and throw a nuclear missile at your funny shuttle, which looks like soapbox.

"I've got you fair and square in my gunsight. Right after that, the Moon, which used to be your home, will follow suit—it'll be demolished. The ISS as well, maybe, if I'm still in the mood for that, but can't see why not, he-he.

"I've also got wind of the fact that Tom and Donna Starling are related to Lianne, your adopted daughter, the bitch. As for Gary and Brenda, I haven't decided yet, but don't worry I'll come up with some brilliantly ingenious ideas, unless they're ready to serve me unconditionally, which I doubt.

"However, they'll be given a choice, because I'm strict but just, as you can see. You blew all your chances, anyway. It's too late for *your* lost souls."

"Dixon, don't insult Princess Lianne, alright," Brian requested.

"And now what, you wanna be a knight, then? That's so outdated, my bratty brother."

"Right, but may I just add something finally, Dixon?" Peter inquired.

"Go ahead, that would be your last word indeed, old thing."

"Only a quick note to Brian first. Brian, my boy,

you're a brave and honorable young man like General Grant, when he was young. However, your self-sacrifice won't help us in any way, unfortunately. Dixon's really obstinate, I know him quite well," Peter started.

"Well done, you have some common sense then. There's no point in contradicting me," jeered Dixon. "But don't even mention the General, as he may be the worst traitor and telltale of all. I assume he'd given away all the details of our secret mission to you, right Peter?"

"No, Dixon, you're wrong. Don't be stupid. I'm not like you. I have technologies that are much more advanced and sophisticated than yours, you know that. So please don't blame Mr. Grant; he's loyal and dignified."

"Fine, fair enough, I see your point, but do you have anything else to say before I send you off to eternity? Pray for your rotten souls and hope that there's an afterlife, as you're all poor losers, nobody, damn rubbish."

"Listen, Dixon, let me show you one more thing, something out there in space, only about ten miles away from your spaceship, just off the ISS. Can you see that mini meteoroid, merely a few yards in size?" Peter prompted.

"So, old man, is that one of your stupid bluffs? Do you consider yourself a wizard or a magician? What on earth are you gonna do with this funny stone? See what I can do with it first. No one could stand up to me."

Then Dixon pointed the laser cannon at the little meteorite-like body, took aim, and fired with alacrity and contentment.

Several seconds later, the astronomical body, that is, the little rock, broke into small pieces, flames bursting all around; then, only dust and a waft of smoke remained.

Eventually, there was nothing left of the stone, just sheer blankness, as though the latter had never existed.

"Did you see that, Peter? That's you and your friends in a minute," rejoiced Dixon.

"Yes, I did, Dixon, very well. You didn't even bat an eyelid. But believe it or not, only a couple of minutes ago, a tiny splinter—merely a few inches wide—was chopped off the meteorite that you blew up. It's gained speed rapidly and is currently heading toward your spaceship," Peter explained.

"You're talking nonsense again, old lunatic. For your information, my high-tech radars and protective shields would've spotted and destroyed it automatically by now," Dixon assured him.

"Maybe, but since it's so small, they might've missed it. Size does matter, you see. In other words, small is big.

"Anyway, it's already caught fire, there's a little flame at the end of its tail, due to its extremely high velocity. It actually represents the perfect bullet.

"So, Dixon, this is your last chance. I implore you to stop now, otherwise—"

"Otherwise *what*? Don't gimme this shit. I've had enough of your slush. So, I'm pressing the button this instant."

Dixon's hand moved toward the button and as he was about to press it, there was an unexpected whistling sound, and something small swooshed by like a fiery bullet.

By the look of it, a tiny burning pebble had gone through the front window of the cockpit, melting it and leaving a small crack behind, hardly visible at all. It had obviously taken its pre-programmed course and ended up in Dixon's chest, right where his heart was supposed to be.

The only thing Dixon was able to do right after was whimper and groan. "Damn you all, see you in hell, Brian and Peter."

He continued writhing in agony on the floor. Then, something hideous appeared right over his body. It looked hazy, but had the shape of a monster, a demonic creature, quite bizarre and outlandish, which shrieked horrendously and eventually disappeared.

"He was definitely possessed. That can't have been your brother, Brian. Allegedly, he had a heart of stone, which wasn't in the right place, anyway. Such a small splinter made a great difference for humankind, a giant leap, I'd say." Lianne's gentle voice finally pierced the grave silence, which had set in after the bloodcurdling scene.

The control room and the adjacent lounge on Dixon's spaceship started filling with smoke, fumes and dust, due to the decompression caused by the tiny hole in the front window, which was in flames. The radiation sensors were activated accordingly.

For safety reasons, all crew members had to transfer immediately to another part of the spaceship. Dixon's dead body lay lifeless on the floor, already charred and almost unidentifiable. His body had been transformed into an amorphous mass in a matter of minutes.

[17]

MORE THAN 10 MINUTES HAD ALREADY PASSED. However, no matter how hard they tried to get in touch with Dixon's spaceship, Peter's crew wasn't able to receive any news or signal from the latter.

"Hurry, we must go there as quickly as possible and see if we can save the people onboard! We have to avert an explosion, as this is a nuclear ship, a very dangerous one," Peter instructed anxiously. "Go on John, speed up!"

"Calling the ISS, can you hear me down there?" John asked urgently.

"Yes, captain, how can we help?"

"We need your urgent support and backup. Please send your SWAT team, sappers and combat engineers to Dixon's spaceship asap, speed is vital. We'll meet you there," John stated.

"Copy that captain, we're on our way. We shall be there in less than five minutes, so stay on the line."

Lianne, Peter and Brian seemed tense and furtive, as if they were afraid of what was going to happen next. The spaceship in distress was already in sight. The five-minute journey felt like eternity.

———

Having moved to the Emergency Control room, the crew were in relative safety. However, the on-board computer was out of order and all major systems didn't seem to be functioning properly. In fact, the ship was aimlessly free-floating. There was no communication with the outside world—no video or sound connection.

———

"Captain Daniels, let's send out a distress message again," General Grant ordered.

"What do you think you're doing, General?" Vince inquired. "Who said you're in charge now? I'm the minister and our mission isn't over yet. Our target's still out there and we must complete it, no matter what."

"Vince, be reasonable please, the President's dead; we're in danger and need to save our own lives. Can't you see the seriousness of the situation?"

"I see, General, but I'm the boss now and you don't have a say here, understand? Fire the atomic cannons Captain, that's an order."

"Vince, stop, I can't allow that," the General insisted.

"Says who? Who the heck are you, General? You and your friends betrayed the President," Vince retorted, moist-eyed. "It's time to get even with you. I'll start with you first." Vince took out his gun and pointed it at the General.

"Vince, have some dignity—don't you think you should surrender? The ISS guards are on their way and will be here any minute now. There's still a chance for you," the General declared.

"You're so old-fashioned, General, and such a gentleman. Just look at you, he-he. Shame, you ain't gonna live for much longer."

Vince was on the point of pulling the trigger, without any remorse, when the General swiftly removed a commando knife from his trouser pocket and stuck it into Vince's chest.

Despite being taken by surprise, Vince instinctively fired his weapon several times. The bullets pierced the General's torso.

Although fighting for breath himself, Vince was able to hear the General speak with enormous pain.

"We're even now, Vince, so rot in hell!"

"See *you* there, you stupid son of a bitch!"

A few moments later, Vince's eyes were wide open and still.

"Quick, let me help you, General."

"Listen Jeff—Jeff Daniels, you're the commander now. Here are the ship's security codes." General Grant pointed to his right pocket. Jeff retrieved a bunch of electronic chips, smart cards and USB flash drives, containing top secret information, including the launch codes for the nuclear warheads, the so-called Gold Codes.

"Promise me one thing Jeff, make peace, not war," General Grant requested.

"I certainly will, General, you have my word, sir."

The General didn't reply after that. His soul had apparently ascended to another world. His body was already motionless, but there was something inexplicably magnificent about his appearance, even after he had passed away.

"OK everyone, listen to me—are you all on my side?" Captain Jeff Daniels addressed the spaceship crew as the newly appointed commander. "You heard the General. Does anyone object? I'd like to know," he reiterated, still not sure how to proceed.

"We're all with you, Commander, as the President, the Minister of Defense and the General, the Commander-in-Chief, are all dead now. At your service," replied some of the officers.

The rest followed suit with affirmative statements and congratulations, despite the fact that some of them used to be Dixon's or Vince's supporters. They were obviously unprincipled, but afraid to oppose anyone now that their evil masters were both gone.

"Great, follow me then and you shall live, I promise," encouraged Jeff. "But first, let's neutralize those damn nukes and try to restart the spaceship."

Right then, as if by magic or a strange twist of fate, the major systems of the spaceship started to work properly again.

"Smashing, the ship's now in order, so let's get out of this potential graveyard. I must lead you to safety, my folks," stated Jeff with an affirmative nod.

"Hello, can you hear us? We're right beside you." Peter's voice could be heard again and his face reappeared on the wide screen.

"Yes, Governor, I hear you loud and clear. I can also see you quite well, thank goodness. We seemed totally lost just a few minutes ago. By the way, my name's Captain—I mean, Space Commander Jeff Daniels."

"I know who you are, good man, thank you. Anyway, is everyone all right there on the ship after the breakdown? Hope it's not a total mess after all. How about Minister Brandon and General Grant? What had happened?" Peter asked too many questions all at once.

"Well, Governor, erm, I regret to tell you that, errr, they are—are both—dead, so to say, sorry indeed."

"What? Did I hear you right, Jeff?" prompted Peter.

"You see, we had a situation in here, which really got out of hand. To begin with, the Minister insisted on continuing with the mission, whereas the General stated that it should be aborted by default, after the President's death.

"Then, the Minister took out his gun and shot the General. However, the General reacted instantaneously and combated the Minister with his army knife. The result is known, as I reported earlier. Everything's recorded as well, in case you want to investigate further."

"Poor old General, he was a dignified man. He sacrificed himself to save us all. We shall remember him, and he should be interred with military honors, by all means. But damn bloody Vince, the bastard; I would kill him again if I could!" replied Peter angrily. "Now, Jeff, please excuse me. I got a bit emotional, which is understandable under the given circumstances."

"We're all gonna miss him, Governor, he was a great man, a hero indeed. General James Grant—a name to be remembered. This is an inconsolable loss. I think he was like a brother to you."

"That's right Jeff, thank you. Now, could you follow us carefully? Is the ship fully operable? We urgently need to inspect it at the ISS, for we can't run any further risks with the deadliest weapons onboard. Do you copy?"

"Yes, certainly, sir. May I ask something before we embark on this journey?"

"Of course, my friend. So, is everything alright down there? How about staff morale? If you need any assistance, just shout," Peter instructed.

"Ah, yes, everything is under control; all the officers are ready to serve us. However, I'd like to thank you, sir. I saw everything and therefore should say you've just averted a nuclear apocalypse today, a potential extermination of the human race. Congratulations, Governor! We're all at your service now."

"Thanks Jeff, I appreciate that, but the merit's not exactly mine, you see. Can't you accept the fact that it was merely an accident, I mean, the thing that happened to the President? It's already been registered, filed and archived as such on the Moon," explained Peter.

"Yeah, right, as you say, I fully understand, whatever," Jeff grinned.

"Anyway, let's hurry up now."

SEVERAL HOURS LATER

"We were dead worried about you, my love," Donna told Lianne when Peter's shuttle arrived at the ISS.

"Hi, Auntie, let me introduce you to Brian. Brian, this is my sweet Aunt Donna."

"Glad to meet you, Mrs. Starling. I'm so grateful to you and your husband for every effort you've made while looking after me in order to save my life and restore my shattered health afterwards. Grandpa Peter told me all about it, thanks."

"Oh, don't mention it, my boy. How do you feel now? Much better I hope?"

"Very well indeed, thanks to your wonderful niece Lianne as well."

"Hey, I'm Tom, by the way."

"Nice to meet you too, Mr. Starling. Sorry, I haven't met you before, I mean, at least not while I was awake. But I've heard a lot of nice things about you and your lovely wife," replied Brian.

"You're always more than welcome here. I'm so happy you've met Lianne. I think you're gonna make a great couple, although you're already a bit old for

her, my boy, but that's life, isn't it?" Uncle Tom smiled.

"Didn't I tell you to keep your tongue behind your teeth, Tom? You're much older than me too, stupid," Donna scolded him.

Brian blushed and said shyly, "I'd be honored to be the man beside Lianne. However, I feel so inferior to her, I'm so unworthy really. That would be a huge responsibility as well.

"At the end of the day, she and Grandpa Pete saved the world, my own life again, and I—I did what? Nothing, that's it," he faltered.

"Oh, I'm sure your time'll come one day too, my son," Donna interrupted.

"That's not true, Brian," Lianne retorted and then turned toward her aunt and uncle. "He was actually ready to sacrifice his own life today in order to save ours, together with our nice little home, the Moon, I mean. He's already our hero as well."

Brian tried to object. "I'd never put it that way, but—"

"So, isn't it time you popped the question and proposed to your lady?" Peter interrupted, gesturing.

"What, on my knee, *now*? Ah, yes, of course! Lianne, I assume now's a good time, in the presence of your family and relatives. I'm sorry, but my immediate family are all gone, except for Grandpa Peter, whom I've only recently rediscovered.

"What am I talking about? I think I'm making a complete fool of myself right now—even without the temporary speech impediment I had after the accident, when most of my front teeth were missing."

"Brian, the question," Peter reminded him.

"Don't push him. You're all very tired, even knackered, I suppose, after this eventful day, which has been fraught with danger. You may want to have a good rest first in our luxurious space resort, and sample our invigorating refreshments, right?" suggested Donna.

"No, wait, I'm not a coward at least. I think I'm

ready—now or never, as they say." Brian managed to cut through the indecision and seemed much more courageous and self-assured.

"Oh, yes, finally. Are you really sure, Brian? That would be an incredibly risky step, you know?" Lianne teased.

"Right, Lianne, I should admit that we didn't actually have much time to get to know each other very well, but I really mean this now. Lianne, will you marry me? To tell you the truth, I'll be the happiest man in the universe if you say yes. So, what do you say, my love?" Brian rambled, his usual manner of speaking.

"And what was the question again?" Lianne was trying to win some more time before answering. "OK, that was a joke, of course. But as you really mean it, and coz you seem like a decent old man, I'd go for an affirmative answer and say—why not, Brian? Yes, yes, yes, my man!" Lianne radiated with a brilliant smile.

All the people around them started applauding loudly and cheering joyfully.

Warm and sincere congratulations ensued.

———

Peter took out a small box, opened it, and revealed an exquisite gold ring with a precious colorful stone that resembled a diamond.

"Now, that's official," stated Peter after a moment of silence. "Here, please take this ring, Brian. It once belonged to your granny; now I'd like you to offer it to your fiancée and future wife Lianne."

Lianne's eyes sparkled. Brian felt so awkward again, not knowing what to do or say next.

"Now, before we proceed any further, please forgive my previous absence, which was due to some objective obstacles that are now eradicated, thank goodness! I've always been your family, young man, don't ever forget that."

"From this moment onwards, we shall be your family as well, our dearest boy," Aunt Donna added.

"That's all very nice, but we're gonna have a proper wedding ceremony, with a reception and all that in a few days, aren't we?" Tom added.

"Of course, my hubby. Everyone's invited."

The crowd cheered once again, rejoicing.

Tom wrapped it up. "And now, all drinks and nibbles are on the house, so please help yourselves and join us."

The young couple kissed affectionately, apparently not so interested in the food and drinks being served around them.

Everyone seemed content, approving and rooting for them. It was a much needed break from the dark days of Dixon's deplorable tyranny. The days that now seemed to have ended, hopefully, and the rule of law was about to be restored.

Dixon's story had hit the headlines: the leitmotif being "The World's Most Appalling Tyrant Killed by Aliens?", as well as "The Cruel Dictator Beaten at His Own Game!".

[19]

ONE WEEK LATER

"DEAR FELLOW CITIZENS, WE'RE GATHERED HERE today to commemorate the heroic deeds of General James Grant, who gave his life in order to save our world.

"He was a great and honorable man, together with his niece, Alice Gardner, who also fought against the previous dictatorial regime. We shall always remember them.

"Something more, hadn't the General sacrificed his own life, perhaps we wouldn't be standing here with you today. Therefore, we're so indebted to him. Lest we forget!"

Those were the opening lines of the Governor's speech in the ISS Central Conference Hall. Several hundred people attending the ceremony stood silent— their heads bowed, tears rolling down. Afterwards, a three-day mourning period was announced.

As for Dixon Sunderland and Vince Brandon, they were buried quietly and inconspicuously; no one shed even a single tear for them. They were doomed to eternal oblivion.

———

Ten Days Later

After the official wedding ceremony, Tom and Donna congratulated the newlyweds once again and Donna told them, "We're so glad for you indeed, dear kids. You're such a lovely couple. Wishing you a long and happy life together, and a few sweet youngsters of your own soon, when the time's right, of course."

"Actually, our wedding present for you will be a honeymoon on Mars. You're gonna see your good old friends Gary and Brenda there. Unfortunately, they couldn't make it here on such short notice. However, I'm sure you'll catch up with them very soon," Tom added.

"Thank you so much, indeed. You're really like our own parents," Lianne and Brian replied simultaneously.

"Safe journey," Peter wished them. "And don't forget to come back in a month's time, as we have so many issues to resolve concerning the world's governance going forward. But, for the time being, please relax and enjoy yourselves, my beloved grown-up children."

Soon after that, the young couple set off on their journey to Mars, together with Captain John, who also acted as Brian's best man. The journey itself was going to take a whole week. Nevertheless, they were really looking forward to it. Love was in the air and the Sun was shining so brightly, as if it were beaming with joy.

[20]

THE MOON GOVERNOR WAS ACTING AS AN INTERIM Governor of the whole Solar System, due to the latest dynamic developments on Earth. Peter was awaiting Lianne and Brian, together with Brenda and Gary, in order to decide on the future strategic course of action.

There had to be a special session of the General Assembly organized on Earth, so that some tough discussions and debates could be carried out, involving all the regional governors there. Consequently, all the senators were expected to vote on a proposal for general elections to be held so that all Earth citizens could cast votes in a democratic way in order to elect a new world government. This was something that had not been done in a long time, ever since Dixon, and his father Gilbert before him, stepped into office.

In fact, Dixon was never elected per se. He had been single-handedly appointed World President by his father on his deathbed some 20 years previously. Therefore, all the provinces, states and regions on Earth were subdued and brought under Dixon's control . . . that is, his *despotic* rule.

Many people who dared to resist or speak against that rule openly were exiled to Mars, sentenced to lifetime imprisonment without any court trial, cruelly punished, brutally tortured, persecuted, or even ruthlessly executed.

The Moon Governor, however, was intent on liberating all the Earth regions and deterring such atrocities from happening ever again in his lifetime. He'd seen more than enough of those. Luckily, Mars, the ISS, and the Moon were the frontrunners in democratic change and development, something which Dixon had objected to all the way. On the other hand, Peter Drake had managed to keep him away from the developments in those places.

The fight against Dixon was fierce and cruel, but now it was already a thing of the past. Nonetheless, the battle for Earth governance was not going to be an easy one at all either. Apart from sincerity and openness, it also required clever political and diplomatic moves, smart persuasive tactics, so as to win people's hearts and minds.

In general, people on Earth were highly disillusioned and apathetic, fed up with populism and utopias. They could become potential victims of new dictators and their respective lies. Thus, so much was at stake. Many hopes could be lost irreversibly once again.

[21]

LIANNE AND BRIAN HAD SO MANY THINGS TO SHARE
with each other on the long-haul flight. Time seemed to
fly. Being together was sheer bliss. Captain John and the
flight attendants proved to be lively people.

Brenda was appointed Lianne's bridesmaid for the
upcoming after party on Mars. Gary, on the other hand,
was going to be Brian's best man there, of course—a
"second" one, but that did not matter, bearing in mind
that neither Lianne nor Brian could, unfortunately, attend their wedding on Mars before.

They had chatted several times online, but were
anxious to see each other in person, after so many years
of separation. In fact, Lianne herself had not personally
met either of them yet, but had already become their
best friend by meeting and keeping in touch via the
Internet.

"Brian, you should know that Uncle Pete and I'd
been watching you for a few months prior to the accident on St. Anastasia Islet. As far as I could gather,
Brenda had a crush on you before laying eyes on Gary
and falling in love with him," teased Lianne.

"My dear, please be serious; there was absolutely
nothing between us. Besides, that Brian from there and
then is now pretty much dead, don't you remember? It

was a long time ago, indeed. I feel like that was in a pre-vious life or something. I'm sort of living a second one, a fresh new beginning with you now, my love!" stated Brian with a blissful smile.

"Glad you said that, my hubby. You ought to know I have pretty high moral standards as well."

"Do I detect a hint of jealousy, my darling? Anyway, Brenda and her late friend Alice were on a mission then. At first, I didn't like them at all, to be honest," Brian explained solemnly.

"That's why I like you, stupid. You're *my* man. But the way she was looking at you was like, you know, as if she wanted to, erm, devour you. On the other hand, I didn't like the fact that you started making excuses, you see," Lianne remarked with a hint of sarcasm.

"OK, you win. Therefore, I surrender, as usual; let's drop the subject and go for a stroll to find out if the Sun's still setting—there's such a magnificent view from here, don't you think?" asked Brian, a bit drained from the gentle interrogation.

"Yeah, that's a great idea. Let's go before it's too late," smiled Lianne.

After a while Brian confessed, "You know Lianne, my life was a complete mess before I met you. But then, when I saw you, my princess, for the very first time, you appeared to be a dreamlike vision before my sore eyes. I thought I was seeing an angel in the form of a wonderful lady. I assumed I was in paradise already."

"That's so sweet. I hope you'll still remember those words some 20 years from now, when I get much older and less beautiful, as you might imagine."

"Come on, honey, you're ageless. You'll always stay as stunning for me as you're now. The trouble's actually my age, you see. I already look like your uncle, don't you think?" Brian suddenly started to feel henpecked.

"To tell you the truth, I've always liked older and more mature blokes like you. Not that I've met a lot of them in my life so far. However, you may want to train harder and gain some more muscle mass, as you're still a bit skinny after the accident, not exactly to my taste, you know," jeered Lianne.

"Now, that was a bit harsh, but I'm self-critical and can bear it. I'm definitely gonna work on that, I promise."

"Don't be so sensitive and touchy, Brian. Could you come over here?"

Brian leaned toward Lianne and started snogging her eagerly. Silence was preferred now.

The Sun had already set and the pale face of the distant Moon could be seen on the horizon through the large spaceship windows on the upper deck. So many stars were twinkling as well.

[22]

"Ladies and Gentlemen, this is your Captain John Mitchell speaking. May I have your attention please? Fasten your seatbelts and prepare for landing on Mars."

It was a crisp early morning. The Sun was shining and the view outside the windows was remarkable.

Lianne and Brian's eyes were wide open, full of anticipation, reverence, and excitement.

———

Several minutes after touchdown, the crew members and passengers were welcomed to the Red Planet as VIP guests.

"We're so happy to see you here on our marvelous planet, dear friends," greeted Brenda, vigorously shaking hands with Lianne and Brian in turn.

The two cheerful ladies then embraced each other. Gary and Brian could not help it either and hugged too, in a manly manner, energetically patting each other on the back.

"How was your flight?" asked Gary.

"Very entertaining, thanks to my wife's extraordinary singing skills. She also plays the harp so well. Her virtuosity's amazing," Brian joked light-heartedly.

"I see you had a wonderful time together on the spaceship then," commented Gary with a grin.

"Oh Brian, please stop joking like that, it's so annoying," Lianne chided, then turned toward Brenda. "Anyway, where's your little princess, Teresa? I'd like to see her—been waiting for so long now."

"Of course, my dear, please come home with us—she's with her nanny, having a big breakfast right now, bless her. She's growing so fast, whereas I'm aging in the same way."

"No, Brenda, you haven't changed a bit. And how old is she, by the way?" Brian inquired bluntly.

"Oh, right, you're a flatterer, but thank you, I don't mind a good compliment. Well, our little beauty's just turned four and appears quite clever as well. I think she definitely takes after her mother, you know.

"We actually named her after Alice's mom. If we have a boy one day, we'll call him Philip, after her dad. Oh God, poor Alice, I still miss her so much . . . couldn't actually get over that huge loss, sorry. After all we'd been through together." Brenda's eyes were watery.

"I hope we could be best friends with you too, Brenda. I'm not saying I'd take her place, of course, but . . ." Lianne tried to sound encouraging and hugged Brenda once again.

"Please, excuse my weakness. I'm so happy to see you both. At such times, I always get too emotional, but let's not spoil this happy occasion after all." Brenda wiped her tears, silently appealing to her friends for empathy and understanding.

"That's fine my love, you've also got me by your side. I'm sure our friends understand you, as we *all* miss Alice. However, she might be smiling at our reunion from beyond, you see." Gary gently stroked Brenda's long hair with his strong hands, while hugging her firmly. That usually worked for her.

Witnessing this scene, Brian wondered if he himself would have so much patience and then thanked God his beloved wasn't so sentimental; thus, he didn't have to put up with all that. But then he felt ashamed of his selfishness, recalling his own state of discombobulation right after the coma.

"Let's help you with the luggage and show you around, unless you're too tired and would like to have a little rest to overcome the space-travel jetlag?"

"Oh Gary, thanks, you're so kind, a real gentleman, in fact. However, I'm keen to see the astonishing Martian landscapes," Lianne replied enthusiastically.

"That's right, bro, we'd like to get the most out of our honeymoon here with you, our best pals," said Brian. "By the way, as I said before, you two still look amazing and haven't changed a bit since we last saw each other. Was it five or six years ago, *or more*? I somehow can't get my mental arithmetic right yet, with all those newly acquired human colonies, space domains and territories, numerous time zones and all. It doesn't really bear thinking about—so overwhelming, isn't it?"

"Thanks once again, you're such an old gentleman, but you don't look bad yourself either, considering your recent so-called 'resurrection', as Governor Peter dubbed it. I'm so glad you're alive and well now. So, please, be our guests and do feel at home," Brenda requested.

Lianne frowned upon hearing those statements, having assumed Brenda was Brian's flame previously, as one might have expected. However, she rigorously kept a smile on her face.

"No wonder the Moon Governor's had such grand plans for you, Brian, apart from your dazzling lady Lianne, who's his favorite," Gary remarked.

The latter comment made Brenda squint and appear

sulky, for obvious reasons. "You've never called me 'dazzling', Gary," Brenda scowled.

"OK, let's take it easy guys." Brian tried to soothe the two vibrant personalities. "Back to your point Gary: perhaps I'm the last one to know anything about Peter's intentions. He and my wifey, Lianne, are still keeping me in the dark. Honestly, I haven't got a clue about what this fuss is all about."

"So, maybe ignorance is bliss after all," Gary commented.

"Well, he's invited us all to visit our Mother Earth in a month's time, you know. I guess it would be a heart-wrenching experience in a way—so much nostalgia and pent-up bitterness," Brenda stated.

"Yeah, we'll need to plan our trip at least a week in advance so that we can arrive there in time for the World General Assembly in Paris. Then, Brian, you'll be in the know for sure, huh?" Gary asked.

"So, that means we've got only a couple of weeks left now to revel in your sweet company and discover your outstanding planet." Lianne prompted them to move on.

After the tour, they realized that Mars was completely redeveloped and was now looking magnificent—so incredibly green, sustainable and blooming.

Its infrastructure was immaculate as well. You could see numerous people out and about . . . large pedestrian zones in the cities, shopping malls, entertainment centers, you name it. Life seemed very laid-back and tranquil.

Almost a billion people of all races, nationalities, and ethnic groups were peacefully living on this hospitable planet, together with their pets, farm and domesticated animals, some of which were quite exotic and rare.

Various tourists even ventured to go outdoors, that

is, out in the open, in fashionable protective suits, of course.

Farmhouses and homesteads were widespread and the almost transparent, gigantic biome roofs over their heads were merely accepted or ignored, but diligently maintained.

Lianne shared her thoughts. "By and large, citizens look open, free, happy, lively and creative. Apparently, they feel appreciated and satisfied. Everyone looks exuberant, youngish, energetic, and extremely healthy."

"Most kids and teenagers were actually born here, apart from the constant flow of new settlers, including ex-refugees and their whole families, arriving here in search of a better life," added Gary. "Life seems to be going on, regardless of the grim past. More than five human generations have been living on the planet since the arrival of the first settlers from Earth, some 50 years ago.

"The form of governance is generally called republic. However, the majority of people aren't even interested in politics. Nonetheless, the recent end of Dixon's tyranny was widely celebrated here.

"Not that these people are overly vindictive, but the truth is that most of their ancestors fought for their own freedom and civil rights, paying an extremely high price for that. That's why our society cherishes its liberty so much."

Lianne and Brian were very impressed.

[23]

GARY CONTINUED WITH HIS MINI LECTURE. "Currently, Mars represents a self-sufficient economy, more or less. It's a sustainable one, in fact. On the other hand, its interplanetary trade with the rest of the Solar System is flourishing because diversity is sought after. Export is prevalent, for obvious reasons.

"Most of its fresh organic produce is being marketed as premium goods or luxury items both on Earth and the ISS. Transportation costs are quite high though. Nevertheless, good quality is worth the price; you'll see it for yourselves too.

"As you know, at present, Earth's economy's declining steadily, due mainly to the mismanagement and exploitation carried out by Dixon's administration previously. Hence, millions of people wanted to emigrate and go either to the ISS or Mars. The ISS could not accommodate so many applicants, of course.

"Despite its ongoing redevelopment projects, the ISS current capacity's been estimated at around a couple of million inhabitants, including temporary residents and tourists.

"Besides, the standard and, respectively, the cost of living, are much higher than anywhere else in the Solar

System, so not many people can actually afford to reside there for long.

"Moreover, the Moon itself is a different kettle of fish. At the end of the day, it's a really small but friendly community. Its population's only about two million residents, who are mainly elderly citizens, retired intellectuals, and artistic people.

"Naturally, those people enjoy the peace and quiet there. Some 'well-wishers' tended to call them loners and hermits, surrounded by their bookshelves and libraries with huge amounts of data, archives, mainframe computers, and various databases, storage rooms etc.

"However, there are now also things like spa resorts, health farms, recreation areas, gyms, lecture halls and art galleries. In other words, the Moon's turning into a temple of human knowledge."

"Great, thanks Gary, that was really informative," replied Brian with a quick smile. "Let me add something. As you know, Venus is being rapidly developed as a high-tech park, an advanced R&D space center, a scientific laboratory, where Dixon's nuclear spaceship was escorted to—a high-risk activity in itself.

"Captain Jeff Daniels led the dismantling operation, including several atomic cannons, in a specially designed breaking yard."

"Look what smart guys we've married Brenda, they're so sweet," added Lianne humorously.

Brian thanked her with a wink and continued. "As Peter said, numerous bright scientists, together with their families, have been settling there lately. So, for the time being, just over a million people reside on that planet, despite the latter still being under-researched and largely uninhabited.

"It's a rapidly developing high-tech place with lots of opportunities, an advanced society, so to speak. Hence, the standard of living's also relatively high.

"There are already children that have been born

there, unlike their parents, who were born on Earth and still feel somewhat nostalgic," Brian finished.

"You've definitely got the gift of the gab. It seems like you're ready for your future post," teased Gary.

Brian looked perplexed and was about to ask another question when he heard the following words:

"Shut up, Gary. Not *now*. Please bite your tongue, will you!" interrupted Brenda.

Two weeks passed so quickly that the honeymooners wished they could stay a bit longer.

Brenda and Gary had arranged for some of their associates to take over during their one-month business trip to Earth.

"I can see Peter's point, but as far as I'm aware, there are still very strict regulations in place concerning Earth visits, isn't that right?" asked Brian.

"Well, yes and no. Those regulations don't apply to governors, I mean, not exactly. We need a formal invitation, at least. However, in case of emergency, we can go without the latter," Gary duly explained.

"OK, I understand, we all have invitations from Peter now. However, you and Brenda are governors, Lianne's his official Secretary General, apart from being my wife.

"So, what's my role in all that? Who am I exactly? I'm starting to lose my patience now, you see, bro." Brian desperately needed some clear answers.

"Oh, don't be silly, just calm down. You know what Peter's like; since he's already invited you formally, all the details have been thought out, so don't worry.

"Moreover, I'll be sitting next to you in order to

help you stand your ground, in case some ill-wishers attempt to slight you in the General Assembly hall."

"Thanks Gary, you're his best friend, indeed. Brian'll definitely need your help, considering some of Dixon's 'fans' are still around—they're really fierce haters, opponents from hell, so to speak," interrupted Lianne, upon overhearing the boys' chat.

"Yes, that's what I'm telling him, Lianne. Don't worry, Brian, I know exactly how you feel. Brenda and I haven't been to Earth since we met. But we're actually looking forward to that. It's our birthplace after all.

"Moreover, you won't be alone; we'll be by your side. I'm convinced that Governor Peter has something outstanding in mind for your future. You aren't gonna be just a visitor there, trust me," Gary reassured him.

His friend's commentary actually buoyed Brian's confidence. After experiencing and surviving inevitable death, Brian didn't want to cock up things again.

However, he had to face up to the fact that what was meant to be would be, despite him not knowing exactly what that thing was going to be.

So, he felt he had to be valiant and dauntless. He could not possibly look like a wimp next to his fascinating and admirable wife. He already had somebody to look after, worry about, and live for.

He could not bear the thought of losing it all, once again. In the past, he used to be so self-reliant and lonely that now he felt awkward and uneasy being in the company of so many loving people.

Lianne derailed Brian's train of thought, as if she knew exactly what he was

so deeply absorbed in. "Brian, from now on we shall live our life together; don't you think that's brilliant? We'll depend on each other, my dear prince."

"Hmm, yes, indeed, my love, thanks. It seems I can't do without your helping hand, my darling. I cannot forgo your support. I used to think I'd never need anyone else's help in my life.

"However, when you're around, I desperately wanna be strong and powerful. Ironically, though, all I'm feeling right now's only weakness and despair, and I dunno why. Anyway, sorry to bother you with my gloomy musings.

"By the way, Peter hasn't ever told me you could read other people's minds, like him. If it's really so, I'll be in trouble, right?"

"Take it easy, Brian. Together we can be much more powerful. Basically, you should commit yourself to our relationship and love. I can sense that you're still a bit dubious, but please relax; that's usual for men.

"I know what you've been through since a very young age. You'll fulfill your destiny when the time's right and you're ready, no matter how many adversaries you're surrounded by. Your day'll come soon," Lianne assured him, looping her arms around his neck.

"Spot on, my princess; thanks for your kind words. They make me feel much better already."

Brian felt great power and energy flowing through her gentle hands. He wanted to remember when and if he had experienced anything similar in his life so far. To a certain degree, maybe in his mother's arms, when he was still

a little boy. However, not with such intensity.

Their love was really incredible, incomparable, unmatched, possibly karmic and eternal. Somehow, time and space were starting to loosen their grip in its presence.

[25]

THE TWO YOUNGISH COUPLES ARRIVED A DAY EARLY, just in time for the official meeting. Thus, they were able to enjoy the Earth's atmosphere and adjust to its climate beforehand.

They were breathing in the fresh morning air with delight—unlike the artificially filtered and conditioned one elsewhere. In fact, they were already fed up with the gags and masks, as well as the protective gear against space radiation and cosmic rays, while spending time outdoors on Mars.

They just realized how much they had been missing the natural oxygen on Earth. They were excited and expectant as they were filled with sweet memories. Despite the nightmares and ghosts of the past, they immediately felt strongly attached to this planet again. It seemed like the perfect union.

Their accommodation comprised comfortable business-class hotel rooms.

The next morning, they once again relished the spring sunrise. Some songbirds could be heard in the distance, despite the city's hustle and bustle. Nature looked and sounded so pleasant and welcoming.

It was time to leave for the conference room. They weren't allowed to see Peter until the opening session, for all delegates had to go through extremely strict security checks and countless administrative procedures.

The lobby was buzzing with various kinds of people: journalists, paparazzi, security officers, receptionists, information guides, PAs, other delegates and MPs, political figures, business people, celebrities, VIP guests, some alleged spies, busybodies, etc.

———

"Ladies and Gentlemen from all corners of the Solar System, good morning to you all. Dear delegates, we're gathered here today to elect a new world government, as you know," Governor Peter kicked off, acting as chairman, apart from serving as interim world governor.

His talk was upbeat and concise and he finished on a positive note with the following key phrase, "So, after all, I firmly believe that our best is yet to come. Now, let's proceed as per the agreed agenda."

Brian was not quite prepared for all the long-winded speeches, ramblings and debates, held afterwards by various senators and reps.

Then the assembly meeting continued with three consecutive plenary sessions, including a few coffee breaks in between. Finally, it was time for the long-awaited lunch break. Brian was already starving.

The food in the canteen was actually surprisingly tasty. The canteen itself looked like a galley on a spaceship though. They all needed to recharge their batteries and restore the energy levels after such draining intellectual activities and hard work. Brian was devouring delicious Mediterranean-style chicken, which was an integral part of the classic French cuisine. It included various types of mouth-watering salads and finger-licking sauces.

In the nick of time, Lianne leaned over and, with

fervor, said, "Slow down my love; please don't eat like a pig. Everyone's watching."

"Oh, I'm so sorry! I apologize for my blunder and thanks for reminding me. I guess I still need to learn some table manners and proper etiquette, indeed," responded Brian, blushing.

The people from the adjacent booth started giggling and bantering with each other, while glaring at Brian. Apparently, his bad and uncivilized behavior was regarded as disgusting, even as a misdemeanor.

"Take account of the fact that currently you're neither on the Moon nor on Mars, my man," Lianne added.

Brian felt like a real outcast. He'd already owned up to his mistake but thought it a bit too harsh, if not over the top. He started questioning himself: would he match up to Peter's expectations?

Needless to say, he lost his appetite. His confidence was blown to smithereens again; the poor waif was in a quandary about how to move on. Feeling uncomfortable, he tried to keep the awkward conversation going.

"So, after all, what are we here for? I still couldn't get the gist this morning. Are they gonna make some clearer statements this afternoon? The next few days are likely to be damn boring in that large hall, don't you think so, my darling?"

"Brian, my baby, you look like an angry kid; hasn't anyone told you this before, huh? You'd better get ready for your big speech tomorrow. Then, you need to look far more convincing, presentable and authoritative. Ya know, Uncle Pete has bet on you, so don't let him down, my man." Lianne's words were startling.

"What speech?" Seething, Brian's voice wavered. "What the hell am I supposed to talk about in front of all those stuck-up snobs inside that hall? I can't. I'm awful at giving speeches, let alone persuading or selling ideas or whatever."

His angst was visible. Droplets of sweat were welling on his forehead.

Lianne just smiled and added, "You can make it, my knight; you will, I'm sure. Otherwise, you're gonna lose everything you've gained so far and you'll be nobody again. That used to be your usual state, right?

"You don't wanna go there, believe me. Your future'll be precarious, to say the least. I can see you're encumbered with fear, doubts and worries, but please be a real man, Brian, be my hero from now on, please."

Brian was trying hard to remain calm and not lose his cool. He also gathered he might come across as a dyed-in-the-wool bozo. "Your support gives me warm fuzzies, my love. It's so comforting, thanks very much."

He sounded defensive again and tried to ward off the verbal attack, but looked very glum and unyielding. Obviously, his stubbornness got the better of him.

Assessing the situation, Brian stepped back. He definitely did not want to lose the lady he had recently started a family with, the one he truly loved and was ready to die for. He picked up where they left off.

He rallied and continued. "Sorry, Lianne, I'm so stressed out these days. But, anyway, could you please give me a hand tonight with my speech preparation?"

"I'll think about that, my man, maybe. But don't forget that you'll have to do it yourself tomorrow. I mean, giving a presentation, the oral defense afterwards, taking tough questions and all."

"Hey lovebirds, how's it going here? Is the food good? How do you find this place overall?" asked Gary in the way of a greeting, Brenda standing next to him.

"Ah, yes, thanks for asking. The food's really tasty; come and join us. The afternoon session's starting in less than 20 minutes, so we need to be quick."

"Brian has to conquer his stage fright with a view to giving his speech tomorrow," teased Lianne.

"My bro, don't chicken out. Brenda and I'll be first,

just before you, right after Peter's opening lines. We'll prepare the ground for you, so don't worry. You'd better think of some witty answers to the stupid questions by the opponents, journalists, haters and trolls," laughed Gary.

"I appreciate that, my friends. You may laugh at my expense . . . take the mickey out of me . . . making fun of my failure and public humiliation tomorrow."

"No, no, I'm sure you'll be fine. Lianne'll be talking prior to your presentation. Then, Peter's gonna make a formal introduction to announce your nomination. So, your talk will follow on from there," Brenda said encouragingly, trying to assuage Brian's nervousness.

The bell for the afternoon session rang and they skipped the sweet desserts.

"OK, then, so let's hear the verdicts, that is, our nominations. Not that I've got an inkling of what they're for, anyway. But for Peter, I wouldn't even bother. Let's hope, although I doubt, it's gonna be all smooth sailing," Brian said mockingly.

[26]

SUFFICE IT TO SAY, THE AFTERNOON SESSION WAS much more exciting and eventful compared to the morning one.

In a nutshell, the nominations for the post of Earth Governor were already quite a few when chairman Peter Drake spoke again. "Dear all, as an acting interim world governor, let me introduce to you Ms. Lianne Starling, my nominee for the position of Governor of Planet Earth.

"I believe she's mature enough to take over from me and rule our world wisely, caringly, justly and responsibly. I'm certain that she can lead the world society to peace and prosperity, by eschewing all forms of violence, and ultimately, reversing the downward trend of current development caused by the mismanagement of the ex-president, Mr. Dixon Sunderland's administration.

"Moreover, despite her relatively young age, Ms. Starling's well educated, capable and skilled at dealing with social affairs, as well as crucial state matters, having served for over a decade at my lunar central office as a vice-governor.

"In fact, her expertise and sound reasoning proved invaluable. Therefore, I back up her application with my personal reference, which is also acclaimed by all lunar elders. Now, let's proceed with the actual voting process."

All delegates then cast their votes.

Several minutes later, the chairman spoke again. "The voting's over now. Thank you all very much. Now, as per the agenda, I'm gonna read the results. The candidate that has got the highest number of positive votes is Ms. Starling. She's won nearly 80 percent support, a whopping figure by all means, so my hearty congratulations! I'd like to wish her every possible success."

Lianne was given a standing ovation.

"And now, on to the next item on the agenda. I'm happy to welcome the governors of Mars, Mr. and Mrs. Scholes. Looking forward to hearing your progress reports and presentations. The floor's yours."

The couple was warmly applauded. People in general respected them, because Mars was the fastest growing and the most sustainable human colony in the Solar System. Its poverty rate was among the lowest as well. Moreover, the previous year, the planet was voted the best place to live.

Notwithstanding that they were people's favorites, Brenda and Gary kept their speeches brief and succinct. They never failed to move the audience—their talks were always incredibly convincing and down-to-earth, not to mention their candor. Afterwards, they were both re-elected for another five years.

Right after their speeches, General John Mitchell, the lunar Commander-in-Chief, was proposed as the First Governor of Venus. Soon after that, he was unanimously elected. A historic step in itself. As he was an outstanding

aerospace engineer, his skills and expertise would definitely come in handy when governing such an enormous high-tech park on the planet.

He also had to assign his associates and organize a

local government with the appropriate committees, agencies and administration. In fact, he was the only suitable candidate for this responsible post. John gave a brief but candid speech as well, promising welfare, prosperity, sustainability and appreciation to his fellow citizens.

Congratulations ensued from all corners of the Plenary Hall.

Then, a 10-minute break was announced.

ONE DAY LATER

HAVING LISTENED TO HALF A DOZEN OTHER candidates, the chairman finally summoned Ms. Lianne Starling to appear in front of the audience.

"Good afternoon, everyone," greeted Lianne. "I'm ready to take your questions."

"Ms. Starling, knowing your background and love for innovation, would you be prepared to work alongside the supporters of the previous World Cabinet? Won't there be a clash between your political line and theirs?" a senator challenged with a smirk.

Most people booed, expressing their disapproval. Lianne had known all along that this moment would come sooner or later. However, she could sense the insalubrious atmosphere and the upcoming shenanigans of the opposition.

"Thank you for this question. I know where you're coming from, but I can assure you that my team and I will gladly work with all those people who long for Earth's restoration, economic boom, and building of a real civil society, based on the rule of law and democratic principles.

"I'd also like to say that there'll be proper sanctions imposed on all criminal circles that want to enslave, exploit, and oppress innocent people, that is, their fellow citizens.

"No form of dictatorship and totalitarianism will be encouraged anymore. Tyranny must never be forgotten but should become a thing of the past, so that our world society could move on and develop peacefully."

Most senators were quite pleased with Lianne's wise answer. However, the same senator that asked the previous question, persisted. "Very well, Ms. Starling, but does that mean that you're gonna seek revenge and re-press all of Dixon's henchmen?"

The audience grew noisy again.

Lianne motioned for the MPs to calm down. "I see your preposterous concerns, Senator, but let me re-phrase my statement in the following way. Of course, deep reorganization and restructuring is long-awaited and needed, but we have to do that in peace, while re-specting each other's rights.

"Justice, on the other hand, should also be restored. Everyone's liable for their own actions. The main mes-sage though is that our ultimate goal should be edu-cating and encouraging all citizens to achieve something beneficial and significant for our society as a whole.

"And, finally, no one must be above the law, despite their rank, connections, influence, etc. The notion of humanity has to be our leading principle. If you allow me a counter-question here: why are you so nervous about divulging the misdeeds of the previous regime? That would be beneficial to all of us; knowledge *is* power."

Her mean-spirited opponents wanted to provoke many more similar petty cavils, altercations, and vile verbal attacks, thus sabotaging the whole inauguration ceremony.

Most people in the room, however, managed to overwhelm their shouts and glaring disrespect with applause. Lianne's words resonated powerfully with the majority of delegates who hankered after real changes and reforms. Some of the obstacles, albeit, seemed insurmountable.

"OK, order please," the chair demanded. "If there are no further questions, let's move on to the next item. Let me remind you once again that everyone's allowed up to two questions per topic, so please observe the rules, ladies and gentlemen—there'll be no exceptions.

"I'd like to ask Ms. Starling to give her inaugural speech now."

"Dear MPs, delegates, representatives, governors, guests, and fellow citizens,thank you all very much. This victory isn't mine, but *ours*. I'll serve you with all my heart, dedication and goodwill. I shall listen to your voice, answer your urgent calls, cater to your needs. Whenever there's a problem or a difficult situation, my office door will always be wide open for you, I promise."

Most people were deeply touched, their eyes moist. That was not the usual Dixon populism, which used to be rife prior to the initial sedition. Thereafter, numerous uprisings followed.

Lianne's words were so heartfelt that she instantly became the people's favorite. Only a few angry faces could be spotted—allegedly, the ones who'd served as Dixon's "goons".

Pursuant to her speech, it was agreed that all human colonies, regardless of their size, would have an equal degree of autonomy, decentralization, proportional representation and participation at the Universal Assembly. Moreover, those territories would be ruled in compliance with the principles of equal opportunities, non-discrimination and human rights. Needless to say, those privileges and rights had been unthinkable only several years before, during Dixon's tight rule and abuse of power.

Brian was dumbfounded at the rapid developments

taking place before his eyes. He had always believed in his wife's excellence but could never fathom the scale of admiration and appreciation she had gained. He felt so insignificant once again. The chasm between his current status and his aspirations looked humongous.

[28]

"THANK YOU ALL VERY MUCH INDEED. TODAY'S BEEN a very productive day so far, dear ladies and gentlemen." The chair did not spare his compliments. "Before we take a break, I have one final but very important announcement to make. Either tonight or tomorrow morning, at the latest, we need to appoint a new governor of the Moon, for I now need to resign.

"Maybe it doesn't show so much, but I'm fairly old. I might live another 100 years or so because, as you know, we've discovered the recipe for longevity and 'eternal youth' on the Moon. Maybe we should patent it and become obscenely rich, right?"

Most people in the hall laughed out loud. Some senior ladies looked wistfully at the chairman, whispering into each other's ears, "He looks so effing young!"

"Thanks everyone. I realize I look younger than my real age. Now, seriously, I'd like to recommend Mr. Brian Sunderland for the post."

Grave silence suddenly set in. Hearing those words, Brian wanted to get a reprieve, to escape—he needed a break. He also sensed that he was heading for unmitigated disaster.

The chairman carried on. "Don't get startled by this fellow's surname. He's far from a Dixon supporter, in fact. His mother's maiden name was Fleming. As you might know, I also used to bear that name for quite some time—my late wife's name, that is."

The crowd started chattering.

"OK, let me finish. Brian's actually my grandson, my favorite one. And yes, he is, or rather *was*, Dixon's brother, I should admit. But who can choose their own parents, siblings or relatives? Can you? I doubt it. Anyway, Brian's totally different."

"Like father, like son. Stop this bloody nepotism, will you?" a deep voice from the backbenches demanded.

"Right, I do understand your concerns. Therefore, let me explain my reasons. All the elders from the Moon backed this nomination. Furthermore, after my preliminary discussions with all major parliamentary groups and committees, I realized that most people here are of the same opinion.

"Nevertheless, taking into consideration the enormous responsibilities of the position, such as: a) keeping the universal records in order, b) making sagacious decisions on the basis of expertise, exerting the power of veto, when necessary, d) giving expert advice, and e) others.

"I'd suggest that we take a break today, and vote on the issue tomorrow; any objections?"

"Lianne's his wife. Isn't that a conflict of interest then?" one of the adversaries protested and was supported by others.

"I see, let's discuss this tomorrow, as I said. Now the session's over, good night everyone," the chair declared.

Brian was in a bad state of mind, disheartened and dejected. It was a matter of life and death for him again. Something he loathed. It was a make-or-break situation. So, he could not help but dither even more than usual. The hours were flitting by though, regardless—as if his time were running out, unstoppably.

[29]

WHEN LIANNE WOKE UP THE NEXT MORNING, SHE expected Brian to be disheveled and grumpy but, lo and behold, this time she was in for a surprise—she could hardly believe her eyes.

He was standing in the middle of the bedroom, dressed and looking smart, calm, composed, and even smiling, somewhat wryly though.

Last night, they lay entwined in each other's arms. As if all the vitriolic comments of yesterday had been swept away with the help of a magic wand. There was no trace of his previous reticence now. There was a significant upsurge in his confidence for some reason, unbeknown to her.

"Are you ready to go back to yonder big hall, my lady? Let's go get 'em!"

"Brian, my man, are you OK? Don't let it go to your head; beware of your latent stage fever."

———

The hearing went reasonably well up to a point, despite the incessant queries pouring in. Brian felt as if he were on the battlefield. He actually felt like a real warrior— fighting his opponents' constant bickering and derision.

He rightly felt he'd actually fought "absolutely pure evil". However, he managed to defend himself remarkably well, all by himself, without the help of his friends, wife, let alone his grandfather. By the end of the morning session, most delegates were fairly happy with his nomination—which was a victory in itself.

Bit by bit, the audience had a change of heart and started to like this chap, despite the opposition's numerous caveats. Some people began to empathize with him.

Then, there was a brief hiatus in the debate.

Brian was not as eloquent as Lianne or Peter, but his speech style was naturally convincing, open and admirable. Even his opponents' attempts to mock and deride him had ceased.

All his past inhibitions seemed to have evaporated. He stood up to his adversaries in a manly manner, so that they appeared weak and defeated. All attempts to hamper his progress were doomed to failure.

He looked as if he had been to hell and back, but somehow had managed to pull through, without detriment to his overall condition, both physical and mental.

Then, suddenly, another vicious attack occurred, aimed at defiling his immaculate reputation.

"OK, we see that we've got another favorite rookie among us today. First off, please excuse my inability to sympathize with this infatuation.

"Sorry, but I regard it as unfounded. I'm eager to know more about his social status and whether he possesses any wealth after all, apart from his so-called intellectual powers or skills and military exploits, which are also debatable.

"We surely wouldn't want a pauper to be in charge of the good old moon, would we? By and large, governance isn't a form of charity, correct? We wouldn't like a poor boy to govern us, right? We could even suspect a case of potential corruption at hand; what else might beggars want, except money?

"Simply more cash, neglecting moral principles; am I right? Let's feed the poor boy, give him some change, some peanuts, and send him to an orphanage . . . send him to Coventry, as they say.

"We should stop wasting our time with this monkey, dear ladies and gents. Just stop this ludicrous farce now! We shouldn't even be talking to this underdog."

The hall was in turmoil. Brian was caught red-handed indeed, or rather with his pants down, off-guard. Not that he was likely to become corrupt, but as for his wealth and social status, the troll's words pierced like a sword. Brian felt as if somebody had jabbed him in the stomach.

After Dixon had misappropriated his mother's real estate—a tiny old cottage in the suburbs of London—Brian owned virtually nothing, in legal terms at least.

On the other hand, he might be able to regain possession of that small property in court, but to do so, he would need sufficient resources, funds, time, and great effort.

So, for the time being, the only thing he could depend on was the love of his wife, grandfather, and a couple of best friends. Something that did not seem enough in that respect.

Brian was at a loss, standing quiet and very humble in front of the staring crowd. Presumably, he had lost sight of what was transpiring.

Then the chairman spoke again. "Right, I assume that matter was gonna come up at some point. Some things are just meant to be, no matter what. So, as an official record keeper, let me explain the situation and read a piece of factual—that is, indisputable—information to you all."

Peter continued referring to legal documents, including title deeds, among others, while displaying them on the wide screen behind him, revealing essential up-to-date facts, figures, and details.

"Hence, Mr. Brian Sunderland is currently the sole inheritor, and owner, of the real estate that once belonged to his deceased mother. The same property that his brother Dixon had illegally taken away from him previously.

"I suspect that was due to the fact that their parents had divorced a long time before and had lived separately ever since, each son with a different parent, respectively.

"Moreover, the elders on the Moon have recently been attesting witnesses to my last will and testament, designating the above-mentioned person, namely Brian, as my only heir and successor entitled to receive all my property, possessions, wealth and funds.

"I won't need any of those from now on, for my days are already numbered. As a matter of fact, being among the first settlers on the Moon, I possess quite a lot of land there, which is now worth billions, not to mention the numerous patents and respective royalties.

"This way, Brian turns out to be one of the richest people in the Solar System. He ain't poor at all. He's worth quite a lot in terms of material wealth as well. On top of that, his wife's possessions aren't to be neglected either—I'd just mentioned that her parents, i.e. Brian's in-laws, who are loaded, I mean billionaires, own the entire ISS, coupled with several top resorts on Earth.

"Nonetheless, he's open-handed and sympathetic. I'm sure he'll be a conscientious governor, who won't be shirking his duties. Having said that, I believe all your concerns, suspicions and doubts are now dispelled.

"Henceforth, any further attempts to damage my grandson's immaculate reputation will be classified as an insult, libel or slander, and dealt with accordingly.

"The most valuable and precious assets he possesses are his kind heart, brave nature, sharp mind and moral principles, despite his not so impeccable manners, he-he. Any objections?"

The whole Assembly stood still—the authoritative and wise words of the Senior Governor revered. All the delegates were looking up to him. Despite his quirky personality and inventions, which were shrouded in mystery, he was highly respected.

"Best of luck to all your family and in-laws then," jeered a nasty, gravelly voice from the back of the hall, as if it wanted to deafen the voice of truth.

The chairman motioned for the audience to remain calm. "Listen, everyone, those were my last words on that issue. Blood's thicker than water, I agree. But now, people shall decide and elect the best governor of the Moon. 'Vox Populi, Vox Dei—the voice of the people is the voice of God.'

"People are the supreme sovereign that can oust or remove from power any governor, if necessary, in accordance with the law, of course. So, ladies and gents, let's look at the final voting results for Lunar Governor from across the Solar System right after the lunch break."

The whole Assembly breathed sighs of relief. The nasty, gravelly voice could no longer be heard.

The group of four friends went to a fancy restaurant in town. Brian was dying for a drink. He was ecstatic about the latest item of news. All his riches came like a windfall, despite his disbelief. He liked the clichéd story of rags to riches so much—it was right up his alley.

He always wanted to eke out a living from hard work, but his luck was sporadic, like the intermittent rain over the Black Sea in summertime.

He even thought of skiving the next session, but that was just a racy idea—he dreamt of spending the rest of the afternoon with Lianne between his arms. He craved her gentle caresses so much.

30

"DEAR LADIES AND GENTLEMEN FROM ALL CORNERS OF the universe, I'm proud to announce the final results. Here they are, as follows: in first place for the post of Moon Governor with almost 90 percent comes Mr. Brian Sunderland. Thank you all for your trust and support.

"Congratulations on your first mandate, Brian! I'm sure you'll live up to people's expectations and won't disappoint them in any respect. By the way, the candidate nominated and supported by Dixon's backers and successors was next to nothing. In other words, minuscule."

Brian's charisma was second to none. Most people in the room could not actually take their eyes off him. Only a couple of delegates weren't happy and snuck out of the room, infuriated. They definitely didn't see eye-to-eye with Brian. Those belonged to the obnoxious secret clique of Dixon's handful of fans.

The chairman tried to keep the ball rolling and moved on to the next point on the agenda, i.e. the freedom of movement across the Solar System for all citizens including, in particular, the abolition of the ban on travel to Earth from other human colonies.

The proposal was accepted in less than half an hour.

The assembly that year passed many good pieces of legislation and worked very productively at any time of day, almost around the clock, thanks to its meticulous chairman.

It appeared as though nothing could hinder its progress. Luckily, things started falling into place, in some mysterious ways, no matter how hopeless they had seemed at the beginning.

31

THREE DAYS LATER

BRIAN AND GARY, WITH THEIR BETTER HALVES, WERE enjoying themselves on Earth, relishing the short time left until their respective departures. They were still assimilating the exciting news and the latest developments. However, the responsibilities were also increasing and were proving somewhat frightening. For example, Brenda and Gary would need to introduce regular flights between Mars and the other human colonies, including Earth.

However, they now had their minds set on something totally different. Namely, seeing Peter in private, at last. They were all looking forward to a nice and quiet dinner with him. Something that would mean a lot more to them than any other gala or party. It was going to be like a birthday bash, at least for Brian—he was starting his new life right there and then.

———

EARLIER THAT DAY
In the Hotel Room

"Brian, my love, what do you think?" asked Lianne, getting dressed.

"Well, I'm eager to know what else Peter has up his sleeve. By the way, are you ready for the formal occasion tonight? It's gonna be a farewell kind of event for some of us. So, in a way, it'll be a bit sad, won't it?

"Besides, how are we gonna carry out our respective duties, when you'll be based here on Earth, whereas I'll be up there on the Moon, without you by my side? I can't bear the thought of separation, you see." Brian appeared seriously concerned.

"Oh, my sweetie, you're such a stupid big boy. I hope you'll keep telling me the same lovely things 10 or 20 years from now. That'll be a really bright future then, ha-ha!

"Anyway, back to your point, you're aware of the latest technologies, aren't you? There must be an acceptable trade-off between our work and family lives, between your job and mine. In fact, we should work in a team, unless you get bored with my company," Lianne stated with a feigned sneer. "In the best-case scenario, we could divide our time between the Earth and the Moon—we'll be moving house quarterly, so to speak. Thus, we'll be spending all our time together. Wouldn't that be wonderful, my love?

"However, if you need a break sometimes, you may work alone, all by yourself. What would you say?" She gazed at him intently and, suddenly, she reminded him of a wildcat.

"Brilliant, my lady, you're so smart. I think you'd make an astonishing female sleuth. You're so much better than me when it comes down to planning and analyzing—things that I can't really stand, to be honest.

"As for getting bored, you must be joking, my baby —there's no chance that I'll ever get bored, I promise . . . unless you do, as I'm such an old prat at the end of the day," Brian teased.

"Nope, no way, my hubby, not at all. Now, you're gonna be my captive animal, my beast for life—there'll be no escape! I'm a bit curious though, if one day you'd like to go astray and fool around with some tarts, for example," Lianne said both humorously and provocatively.

"I wouldn't even think of an escape—that would be the most desirable prison sentence of all. I'd be always enchanted by you and your company, my princess."

"Only by me and my company? Are you *sure?*"

"What d'you mean?"

"Well, we'll be enjoying someone else's company soon as well—"

He looked puzzled. "Whose company?"

"A baby boy's one, stupid!"

"Oh my love, wow, that's awesome! Thank you so much; you're my sexy fairy." Brian hugged and then kissed Lianne passionately and enthusiastically which prompted her to giggled.

Their dream was about to come true.

———

Still lying in bed, Brian asked, "I know it might be a bit too early, but we haven't picked a name for our baby yet, have we, darling?"

"Oh, I have. Don't you think Peter would suit him best?" smiled Lianne, somewhat mysteriously.

"So you mean, we should name our first child after my grandad, right? Yeah, why not? That's the least we can do, in fact—we should express our gratitude to him somehow."

———

"Brian, we need to hurry up. We shouldn't be late; you know it's important."

"Of course, my love, let's go," Brian replied, stopping to admire Lianne's beauty.

She could see that he was reluctant to go right now. She seemed content with the realization that Brian still looked at her with much passion and desire, just like the first time they'd met on the Moon more than a year before.

I'm such a lucky young lady, aren't, she thought.

That note to self was a cheerful one, unlike her next thought, when something gruesome and disturbing dawned on her, which made her face grow sullen.

"What's the matter, my princess? Why are you sad now? Did I say or do anything wrong again? We're setting off in a minute."

"Oh, it's nothing, my man, thanks for asking. It's just a premonition, but we'll find out tonight what Peter's got to tell us. I'm sure everything's gonna be alright in the end."

"All's well that ends well," replied Brian casually. He offered his hand. "Are we ready to go, then?"

"Of course, my knight; let's not keep Peter waiting," answered Lianne with a shining smile, capable of melting any man's heart.

Brian was the luckiest guy, despite feeling desperately horny.

[32]

Brenda and Gary joined them in the foyer of
the fancy downtown restaurant.

The night was filled with flowery smells—sweet,
mellow and appeasing. The cool breeze, coming off the
River Seine, was so alluring and tantalizing, and made
them all feel a bit sentimental.

The four friends were starving, not so much because
of hunger, but because they were full of anticipation.
Otherwise, they were exhausted after the hard work
and the diverse array of emotions they'd experienced
over the past two weeks.

"So, where's Peter then?" asked Brian, ready to binge
on appetizers.

A nearby waiter approached them and replied, as if
he'd overheard the question. "Dear guests, Governor
Peter Drake asked me to deliver this message to you:
after dinner, he'll be waiting for you at the adjacent conference room. There'll be a gala in about an hour. Enjoy
your meal."

So they did, despite the numerous questions still
hanging in the air. They indulged in delicious meals,
noshing main courses and desserts.

On the whole, the candlelit dinner looked very romantic. However, love and sadness appeared to be inextricably linked as well.

[33]

"DEAR LADIES AND GENTLEMEN, THANK YOU ALL VERY much for coming tonight. It was you who made this year's Universal Forum a grand success. An event that'll be remembered for a very long time, I believe. I really hope you'll keep on track in the future as well—for many years to come. So, never let anyone lead you down the primrose path."

Peter, as usual, was serious and authoritative. Twenty minutes later, he concluded with, "As I mentioned earlier, I'm gonna retire from my office very soon. I'm yearning for that now. I guess I deserve it and therefore I'm planning to go somewhere else, where I could relax for good."

Some people started smiling and laughing, thinking that it was one of Peter's usual bursts of eccentric humor. The four friends, however, remained silent and thoughtful, even a little stunned.

"Yes, my dear fellow citizens, I'm sure I'm leaving the universal governance in the best possible hands for the time being. I don't think you'll need my advice from now on, so all the best and please remember me this way."

The guests applauded as the governor left the stage.

In a few minutes, the concierge reappeared and

made the following announcement, "Just before you go home, the governor asked me to read this message out loud, so here it is: 'Dear all, in case anyone wants to ask me a final question, your last chance will be tomorrow morning up until 11 o'clock, in my office, prior to my departure. By the way, the inaugural ceremony starts at 9.00 a.m. and will be broadcast live to all corners of the Solar System. See you tomorrow. Yours sincerely, Governor Peter Drake'. That's the end of the note. Have a good night, dear guests."

Most people appeared saddened.

———

"And I thought Uncle Pete was gonna talk to us in private tonight. I miss him so much already." Lianne sounded disappointed and worried.

"That's really odd that right after the ceremony he wants us to step into office and carry on regardless," remarked Brian, quite surprised.

"Well, Lianne and Brian, I'm sure you're gonna be fine; we'll always be by your side, dear friends. We've already got some experience in governance, as you know," Gary said amiably, trying allay their worries.

"Thanks so much, we appreciate your support indeed. However, the thing that troubles us is what exactly Peter intends to do after he resigns. I know he meant it in a good way, but I didn't like the tone of his message at all, you see," Brian explained.

"We're seeing him tomorrow morning," Brenda jumped in.

"You're right, let's all go home now and get some sleep; it'll do us good," Lianne suggested.

"Sweet dreams then. See you later," Brenda and Gary spoke with one voice.

It was just after midnight and there was a full moon shining brightly over the city.

When Lianne and Brian went to bed, they hugged each other and almost immediately fell asleep, not wanting to foster any ignoble suspicions. They simply wanted to keep their composure and shun negative thoughts. They preferred to dream of their future child, Peter Junior, who was on the way. Their whole life together still lay ahead, after all.

[34]

THE MORNING CEREMONY WAS FORMAL, RESEMBLING A
briefing in a very straight-to-the-point style.

"Once again, congratulations, my dear successors,
my friends. I believe you'll follow in the footsteps of
many dignified men and women before us—people like
General Grant, Annette Fleming, Alice Gardner, to
name but a few," concluded Peter.

———

"Uncle Pete, please, can we just have a word with you in
private?" Lianne asked after the ceremony. She actually
wanted to make an appeal to him to stay.

Peter, however, seemed quite relentless. "Of course,
my children; as I've always said, have patience and when
the time comes, your wish will be granted. Anyway,
please excuse me, I've had such a busy schedule these
days. But now, we can have a chat on the way to the
spaceport.

"Let's bid our farewells properly, as close relatives
and friends," proposed Peter, sensing the tension in
the air.

The two couples were aware of the delicate situation at hand and therefore tried to act accordingly.

"But Peter, aren't we gonna see you again sometime?" blurted Brian, confused and disheartened.

"Look, my kids, you need to understand. It ain't easy for me either, but it'll be better this way, that's life. My only consolation is that you're taking over from me. So be wise, just and merciful. I'm sure you'll manage to achieve outstanding results."

All four friends hugged him, bawling.

"Now, please try to smile and meet your fellow citizens," advised Peter.

Shortly afterwards, they arrived at the spaceport. The doors opened and they entered a huge conference hall, next to the spaceport.

It looked like an impromptu press conference, where all the media attention was drawn to; huge telephoto lenses were trained on them. The audience consisted of hundreds of journalists, reporters, cameramen, interviewers, and the surrounding seats were filled with several thousand spectators. Big screens and loudspeakers were in place as well, broadcasting live to billions of people across the Solar System.

The crowd was waiting.

The information he shared with them sounded as if it came straight from the horse's mouth, as always.

———

Right after the formal ceremony, the people outside the building waited to see the incumbent lunar governor and shake hands with him one last time. He was bound to be remembered as the greatest governor of all time.

[35]

PETER'S WORDS WERE FAIRLY SIMPLE, AND YET QUITE powerful. Every single person understood his message of peace, love and mutual respect. He'd always aligned himself with the citizens.

The latter used to be a hobby horse of his. Nonetheless, most human hearts from all corners of the universe were deeply moved, regardless of their race, walk of life, age, gender, education, wealth, social status, etc.

Mass media broadcast his speech that morning and boasted a record number of viewers and overall rating levels.

Finally, he added, "So, my dear fellow citizens, wherever you are, I'm sure you all want a better future for you and yours—your friends, families and children. Therefore, I believe these young people will prove worthy of your trust, sincere admiration and friendship. After all, power's in your hands, it actually lies within you. I wish you a destiny of happiness and prosperity from now on.

"And please remember the principle of golden mean and moderation as the key to living a good life. Hope to see you again one day, when the time is right. But until then, good luck everyone, and farewell! My heart'll always be with you."

The crowd applauded energetically while the eyes of the viewers in front of a mammoth screen were filled with silent tears.

Most citizens were happy and a bit sad at the same time. Only a handful of Dixon's obsequious supporters were disgruntled and already scheming, as ever, against the backdrop of increasing hopes.

According to hearsay, those coup-plotters wanted to restore the previous dictatorial regime at any cost. However, their ploy was known and couldn't possibly work this time. Somehow, though, those rascals found ways to keep sending out threatening messages. They spoke the language of hate.

Friends wanted to have friends, whereas enemies always looked for other enemies.

All intelligence agencies were on the alert for these psychopaths, inveterate villains. Pre-emptive steps had been taken in order to nip such malicious plans in the bud. Civil society had learnt its tough lessons and didn't want any kind of utopia or populism to rule over it anymore. People, in general, understood the meaning of "dystopia" as well.

Tolerance and broad general knowledge were prevalent, but any antihuman concepts were dealt with properly, by introducing severe legal measures in that respect. Humankind aspired to a higher level of existence, whereas it searched for enlightenment, justice and kindness.

[36]

IT WAS TIME FOR THE ROCKET LAUNCH. THE spacecraft itself looked more like an interstellar starship, equipped with sophisticated, cutting-edge technology. The four friends knew that it was useless to try and change Peter's mind.

Nevertheless, Brian spoke. "Peter, may I ask you a question?"

"Go ahead, my boy, fire away, since this is your last chance."

"Well, Grandpa, you know how much we're all gonna miss you. You're like a father to us. You literally saved our lives. But now, I'd really like to know exactly where you and Pilot John, the Governor of Venus, are heading."

"That's a good question, spot on, indeed. I see you've grown up now and reached the stage of maturity. That's why all the elders on the Moon like you so much. Your knowledge is impressive, my son. So, long story short, let me tell you this thing."

"Yeah, straight to the point, please," Brian insisted.

"Well, you should be aware that right next to our Sun, at the center of the Solar System, there's an invisible, little known and very unstable portal. It connects travelers to distant realms and acts as an opening in time and space, a door into the unknown. Yet, dangerous as it is, that's the only method for me to use now.

"Do you really want to look after a grumpy old granddad of yours, gradually losing his senses and ability to walk, for the next several decades, until the portal opens again or until I die naturally? In either case, you'll probably have to check my vital signs daily," Peter calmly explained.

"But Uncle Pete, how can you say that? We'd be truly happy to spend more time with you for the next 100 years or so. The more time, the better, in fact," Lianne said beseechingly.

"Wait, my kids, please give me a break. It's already heart-wrenching for me to leave you. I've completed my mission, done my duty, paid my dues. I fear that if I stay here any longer, my life will become meaningless and useless."

"Please don't say that," stated Lianne, her expression one of sadness.

"I, too, am going to miss you all so much. But my body's already started to betray me. It'll be a real agony for you and me. Let me die with dignity, while I still can."

Pausing for a couple of seconds to take a few deep breaths, Peter then continued. "In fact, it won't be a real death, not in a classical sense—I'd just go through the tunnels of space and time, thanks to my secret inventions. Then, I'll deliver your regards to Alice, General Grant, and your parents. But I'll still be watching over you, celebrating your future victories, and sympathizing with you in times of trouble.

"I know it's not going to be a bed of roses all the time, but you'll learn fast not to underestimate your enemies—they aren't sleeping, so don't ever forget that. Please grow wiser and stay together, supporting each other. And, last but not least, remember to be humble, all right, my kids?"

"Yes, we will, dear Peter," sobbed the four friends.

"Excuse me, Governor, but it's really time to go now," interrupted John the Pilot.

Peter turned to Lianne. "Oh, and one last thing, Lianne. I do appreciate your sweet gesture of kindness and love, your special tribute. Your future son shall be a great ruler, a powerful but peaceful one, according to the signs in the sky and star positions. He'll be called Peter Junior and Peter II, indeed. I'm glad you're planning on remembering me that way. Thank you, dear."

Lianne's cheeks flushed. Despite her sad eyes, she looked content.

Neither Lianne nor Brian dared to ask how he knew that, but both felt relieved, as they'd wanted to tell him the good news prior to departure.

Then they all hugged and kissed him.

———

When Peter disappeared from sight into outer space, they all stood silent, deep in thought.

After a while, there was a blazing spark right beside the Sun. It lasted only a moment, but what a magnificent moment it was. The Sun looked so bright, as if it were smiling through its fiery tears.

An ostentatious splurge of solar flares could be seen that day. It seemed as though some mysterious sleight of hand was involved.

The great man called Peter was gone forever, and the entire universe was weeping.

Pilot John, the Governor of Venus, returned shortly afterwards. Normally such a journey was supposed to take at least several months at a time. However, it was completed within a few hours that day.

Everyone was focused on Peter's departure and seemed oblivious to the passage of time. People generally perceived him as some sort of magician, a guru, or even a superman. They expected miracles of him.

———

So, John landed at the spaceport in his shuttle, seemingly distraught, bereft, and out of his element. However, this was not due to the flight deck's filtered and conditioned air, flowing through nozzles and orifices. Now he was ready to take the flak: "to dive into the water headfirst".

The four friends were anxious to ask him numerous daft questions. But little did they know what he was about to tell them.

"Well, Peter's final words to you guys were actually written down on a piece of paper. Shall I read them to you?" John asked, then waited for their answers. He looked exhausted, as if he could not even string a simple sentence together anymore.

"Yes, please, what are we waiting for?" demanded Brian.

"Fine, here it is then. Just before I continue, let me tell you one thing. Rumor has is that Peter hasn't perished at all. He's now simply a few thousand light years away."

"Please read it to us!" the others urged.

"OK, what he basically says here is that one day, sooner or later, you'll all be together again, even if he, himself, isn't allowed to come back, of course. Anyway, until that day, he really wants you to enjoy life, to be filled with joie de vivre for an entire lifetime, despite all your troubles—past, present and future. Your welfare should be in proportion to your merits. Enjoyment doesn't necessarily imply gaudy clothes, flashy gadgets and other luxury items, but—"

"Tick-tock, tick-tock. That might've been useful for us at some point in the past, but for now, please move on," insisted Gary.

"Wait, listen, that's important. Always look on the bright side of life and raise your children alike, for you deserve that. You've recently averted a nuclear apocalypse, intended and devised by Dixon and his father Gilbert Sunderland who, regrettably, happened to be my ex-son-in-law—together with their goons. Just remember that.

"In fact, I should thank you all for your self-sacrifice. You'll serve as an example for so many other people who could become heroes as well. That's a huge responsibility." He stopped reading and peered around before continuing. "Therefore, never look down on other people and stand up for the common good. Your four-person team represents the four cardinal directions, so please work together in synergy and try to achieve your full potential."

"Great, those sound like his words of wisdom, indeed. Is there anything else, John?" Lianne asked gently.

"Ah, yes, only his closing lines. Here they are: finally, dear kids of mine, I want you to know how much I loved you all my life. Take care and do look after Tom and Donna Starling—they'll be your parents from now on. Goodbye! Adieu, and please don't be sad. Remember, I'll always be there to cheer you on. That's the end of the note," John concluded and tried to fold the piece of paper, when it burst into flames.

"Ouch!" he screamed, attempting to extinguish the small fire by blowing out the little flames, "It's so hot, it almost burnt my hand."

The four friends, their faces tear-stained, laughed at this unexpected blunder.

"So, did you manage to save the note?" inquired Brenda.

"No, obviously not. It's all gone now, disappeared into thin air. That's one of Uncle Pete's tricks—to fight fire with fire, you see," responded Lianne, pleased that he could still show up around them in various forms.

John cleared his throat and stated, "Actually, I did see, or rather peeked at, the portal . . . or the wormhole Peter was referring to . . . from a safe distance, of course."

"Oh, yeah? Go on," Brian prodded.

All the friends seemed ready to listen very attentively to John's account.

"Well, it looked like a tiny black hole at first, but then the foggy whirlwind cleared up a bit, so I could recognize some of your late relatives on the other side, smiling and waving at you. They were surrounded by some wonderful scenery."

"Alright, but what about Peter? Was he, I mean, is he OK too?" Brian asked anxiously.

"Yes, I could still see Peter. He was a bit closer to me, floating toward them. However, there was already something like a glass screen or ceiling in between, separating our two different worlds. The people up there looked so alive and—young. Oh, I'm gonna miss you so much, old man! Damn it, if only I could go there right now." John wept like a grown-up child.

"Everything's fine, Uncle John." Lianne tried to calm him by hugging him.

Although his story was told in a very simple, even somewhat "brutish" way, all four friends were deeply moved and grew pensive.

"We're all gonna miss Peter so much," Brian commented quietly. "Our lifetime's starting to seem a bit too long now without him. I, myself, can't wait to see all my relatives and friends again."

Brenda nodded. "So true, Brian, but we've got a whole Solar System to look after at present, and that's such a big responsibility, you know. We can't just give up now, at least not yet."

"Oh, no, I didn't mean that, my friends," Brian added solemnly. "I'm not being suicidal here. Far from it, in fact. What I meant was my plan to look into Peter's secret notes and rediscover his advanced technology, so we could find a way to see him sometimes, even from afar. You know, his starship's still with us, thanks to John, right?"

"A-ha, good luck, bro," Gary said, smirking. "Hope you succeed in figuring that out soon, although it looks quite unlikely. Until then, we need to live up to people's expectations."

"Yes, until then, I think I know exactly how to inspire you and help you collect your thoughts, Brian," teased Lianne.

"Wow, I'm glad you two are still considered an item, like in the beginning of your relationship. I wish I could say the same about Gary and me," Brenda said, shaking her head.

"What was that supposed to mean, my love?" Gary

snapped. "I know exactly how to travel backward or forward in time and reignite the spark, even without any special technology or a time machine."

Brian jumped in. "I can't agree with you more, Gary. Love's the most powerful force and easily overcomes any distance, time, or space. I feel my love knows much more about the universe than myself, so therefore, I must listen to her, trying to learn as much as I can."

"A-ha, elementary, professor, but that's why I love you, my man, despite the fact that you're a bit of an introvert and others usually see you as an oddball," jeered Lianne.

"Did you hear that, Gary? You've still got a lot more to learn," Brenda said.

"Alright, you win, I'm just a simple guy, but you know how much I love and care about you, don't ya?" Gary asked defensively.

John held up a hand. "Enough. I'm just glad you're back on track, young lads and lasses. And I'm also glad Peter's now at least happy to be reunited with his wife Bridget."

"I know it takes a village to raise a child, but now, it's only the Starlings and myself who are still around for you. And, after all, I'm only human." He drew a deep breath. "I definitely don't wanna fight with you over the issue of the form of governance in different places, so let's embark on our new life journeys together, everyone. Are you ready to move on and face the music or do you want to stay empty-handed and unfulfilled for the rest of your lives?" Grinning, John clapped his hands together. "Rise and shine, my kids!"

AGAINST ALL ODDS, THE FOURSOME MANAGED TO cheer up and even smile. Knowing they could never get over such an inconsolable loss, they also realized that, ultimately, they had to pull themselves together.

Many VIPs, bodyguards, officials and journalists were already waiting impatiently for them outside, in the lobby. That meant only one thing: their busy lifestyles, full of stress, responsibility, and having to make tough daily decisions were starting right there and then. There was no time to rest, feel sorry for themselves, or mourn the loss of Peter. At least not in public. They needed to appear extremely strong and re-liable, despite their relatively young age.

So, they did. They finally understood a simple fact: that when people help humankind move forward for the sake of future generations, their reward is a sense of well-being and spiritual enlightenment.

Beyond that, these four innocent souls were about to be remembered as some of the greatest heroes of all time. And as for Peter Drake, he was acknowledged as one of the finest minds and philosophers, who changed the course of human history for the better.

☼

THE END

Dear reader,

We hope you enjoyed reading *The Proximity of Stars*. Please take a moment to leave a review, even if it's a short one. Your opinion is important to us.

Discover more books by Benedict Stuart at https://www.nextchapter.pub/authors/boyko-ovcharov

Want to know when one of our books is free or discounted? Join the newsletter at http://eepurl.com/bqqB3H

Best regards,

Benedict Stuart and the Next Chapter Team

For the time being, Benedict J. Stuart resides in Europe with his girlfriend, taking care of two pets. They are still considered to be relatively young and intelligent.

His dreams are mainly about better education, including lifelong learning, raising cultural awareness and improvement of overall human communication worldwide with the help of modern technology.

Finally, he is a firm believer in broad general knowledge per se.

The Proximity Of Stars
ISBN: 978-4-86750-858-9
Mass Market

Published by
Next Chapter
1-60-20 Minami-Otsuka
170-0005 Toshima-Ku, Tokyo
+818035793528

11th June 2021